RUNNING TARGET

ELIZABETH GODDARD

HARLEQUIN® LOVE INSPIRED® SUSPENSE

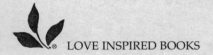

LOVE INSPIRED BOOKS

Recycling programs
for this product may
not exist in your area.

ISBN-13: 978-1-335-23209-0

Running Target

Copyright © 2019 by Elizabeth Goddard

www.Harlequin.com

Printed in U.S.A.

Deliver me from mine enemies, O my God:
defend me from them that rise up against me.
–Psalms 59:1

To Jesus. You're my all in all.

ONE

"Don't move!" Deputy Bree Carrington aimed her newly issued Glock 22 fifteen-round semiautomatic pistol at three men standing in the twenty-four-foot fishing boat.

Though she had the authority of the law behind her, and had trained for a day such as this, her palms slicked and heart pounded.

Inside, she shook.

Still, she allowed her training to kick in, keeping her weapon aimed and level. She never wanted to have to use it, but a sick feeling stirred in her gut—today could be the day when she would have no choice. She pointed the Glock at the three muscled men wearing scowls. Men who made the boat look too small. Men who carried more powerful weapons than she did. Powerful and illegal.

If they got their hands on those...

Well, she couldn't let that happen.

On this hotter-than-usual summer day, sweat beaded at her temples and back.

Next to her, Deputy Jayce McBride tethered the vessels together.

Bree and Jayce had been patrolling the river when

she'd spotted them—just three men out on a boat whose motor had failed on them.

Bree had headed toward them to assist, though the men had insisted they needed no help. But it gave her an excuse to stop and check them out. That's when they had tried to hide that they were transporting illegal arms—machine guns. One guy had grown twitchy and thought he could grab a weapon and take her out. She'd been faster and held them all at gunpoint. If she hadn't, both she and Jayce would be dead.

Now to keep them alive.

That sick feeling continued to churn her insides. This wasn't the way the day was supposed to go.

Minutes before they'd seen the boat in distress, she'd been planning to turn around. It was Stevie's birthday. He was turning five. She and Dad had planned a party.

Jayce, along with his wife of two years, Cindy, and their baby, Taylor, were coming, too.

Instead, she and Jayce were facing off with men who would kill them without a thought.

A chill crawled over her. These criminals had cold, brutal eyes. They were the kind she had never seen before in her line of work in Coldwater Bay. They didn't have the expected look of fear or dread when confronted by law enforcement. Specifically, marine division deputies.

"You two—" she gestured toward the broken outboard motor "—get down on your knees and put your hands on your head."

Jayce would have to step between the unsteady boats.

It wouldn't take much for these guys to shake things up. Rock the boat. Jump into the river that was trying to carry their anchored boat away.

Jayce stepped across and then positioned himself

behind the remaining man standing. Cuffed his hands behind his back. Carefully, Jayce ushered him across to the sheriff's department boat and re-cuffed him to the rail so he couldn't go anywhere.

Meanwhile, Bree kept her weapon aimed at the other two. She'd contacted Dispatch to report their status and tell them that she and Jayce were bringing the men in. She hadn't asked for backup. Backup wouldn't help them in this situation, so far from reinforcements. There were only five full-time marine division deputies, and one of them was off duty today. The other two were on the other side of the county.

She kept her breaths even and steady, staying calm despite the unusual circumstances. Most of the time patrolling the waters was a matter of keeping people safe—performing rescue operations or assisting vessels in distress—not arresting three men who were up to some seriously bad business. If she had to guess, it involved much more than transporting illegal arms. Drug dealers liked big guns, too.

Jayce positioned the second man so that he could cuff him, too. The man bolted to his feet and twisted around to head-butt Jayce. Blood spurted from Jayce's nose.

They wrestled for the weapon and a shot was fired but missed both men. Still, the guy disarmed the deputy.

"Jayce!"

Bree's heart slammed against her rib cage. She fired her weapon at the perp. He grabbed his midsection and dropped the gun, so Jayce picked it up. Her pulse roared in her ears—or was that the ringing sound triggered after firing the weapon?

The uncuffed man who had been sitting scrambled up behind Jayce and caught him off guard.

"Behind you!" She couldn't get a shot in without hurting Jayce.

Before Jayce could react, the man took his weapon away from him and shot him point-blank. He fell back into the water.

Jayce!

Though stunned with profound grief, Bree fought off the shock that would make her immobile.

She fired her weapon at the shooter but missed. In return, he fired off multiple rounds at her as he tried to get to the front of the boat and the machine guns. She dived for cover behind the seat, which was not much cover at all. She couldn't let him get to those guns or it would all be over.

He lunged for the machine guns and she stood to fire.

A shot landed against her chest. Pain exploded, despite the Kevlar she wore under her uniform. She'd bemoaned wearing the Kevlar on hot days, never expecting she'd need it or the life jacket she'd forsaken. She fell back into the river...

And sank beneath the surface. Held the shallow breath she'd caught while more bullets sprayed the water.

Machine gun bullets.

Snap out of it or you're going to drown like your brother! His son, little Stevie, needs you!

The current carried her away from the boat and the spray of bullets.

Jayce had gone into the river, too. Was there any possibility he was still alive? He was also wearing Kevlar. She could hope. After all, like him, she'd been shot and was still alive. Somehow they both had to survive this.

Bree bobbed to the surface and sucked in a breath.

Why weren't the men leaving? Why weren't they escaping in the sheriff department's boat to flee upriver?

A slow-dawning realization squeezed her lungs.

They were searching for her and Jayce, that's why. They had to make sure the two deputies—the two witnesses—were dead and couldn't describe the men who had attacked them.

The uninjured criminal freed the one man who had been cuffed and got their motor running, after all. Maybe they didn't want to take time to transfer their stashed weapons. Either that or they didn't want to be seen in a sheriff's department boat and draw unwanted attention. The boat slowly headed downriver, the men searching the water for the deputies. Underwater, she fought the current and headed for a muddy eddy. Bree's feet found purchase on the pebbled bottom. Catching her breath, she slid forward into the mud. Rolled in it to camouflage herself. She simply couldn't swim away fast enough, even with the river current.

Fear strangled her, making it hard to breathe. Tears choked her throat. She kept her eyes closed as the boat approached. She heard the shouts.

"Find the woman deputy!"

"She's dead. She can't hurt us."

"She isn't dead. She was wearing a vest. I saw her come up for air. The man is dead. Forget him."

Tears mingled with the mud on her face.

Oh, Jayce...

She should have prevented his death. If she'd handled this better, they would be taking in three men and possibly make it home in time for a birthday party. A milestone celebration.

No one would know what happened to them if she didn't survive. Though it took colossal strength, she shook off her grief to be revisited when she was safely away from the murderers.

The sheriff's department knew roughly where they were. But Bree couldn't stay here and wait for the cavalry. She had to move deeper into the wilderness country. Another boat approached, and it wasn't someone from the sheriff's department. She feared for anyone approaching the men—their lives were at stake.

Then when she heard the conversation between them, she understood that those in the approaching boat were more of the *same* men. Partners in crime.

She held her breath and sank deeper into the mud. *Oh, God, help me!*

From her hiding spot, she saw the men transferring to the bigger boat and carrying over the man she'd shot but hadn't killed. She watched to see what they would do next. *Oh, God, please just let them leave.*

Two men hopped onto her boat, then back to the larger boat. They laughed and shouted. An explosion resounded. They'd blown a hole in the hull. Bree watched in horror as the boat she and Jayce had brought upriver sank. The evidence they'd even been here was now hidden away.

Then across the river, she spotted Jayce climbing up onto the riverbank. Her heart surged with hope. *You're alive.*

He rolled over onto his back. Pressed his hand against his chest and to the side. It came away with—was that blood? He was injured, but the Kevlar had still likely saved his life, just like it had saved hers. Only she wasn't bleeding from a bullet. They'd spot him if he didn't move, and he wouldn't live long if they saw him. They thought he was dead. She had to draw their attention away so they wouldn't find him.

Bree drew in a couple of breaths. *You can do this.*

She rolled over and slowly crawled out of the mud. The boat was a mere twenty-five yards from her. Then she made a show of standing up, hoping they would spot her before she ran into the woods.

A shout resounded on the river.

It worked. She ran for cover as bullets pelted the trees. Her only chance was to put as much distance as she could between them, but more importantly, she would give Jayce a chance to survive. Since he was injured, his odds of survival were already slim, so Bree would draw the men away from him.

She ran until she was out of breath, then she dropped to her knees and crawled over rambling mossy roots, well-hidden for the moment within a copse of Sitka spruce and western hemlock. She leaned against a thick trunk and wiped the mud from her face with her arm.

Bree knew the rivers like she knew the lines on the palms of her hands. But the woods? The wilderness area? Not so much. Would her fellow deputies be able to find her? Would they even know the danger they faced in searching if Jayce wasn't able to get to safety and warn them? Other deputies could get shot. Or worse. Die.

Either way, if he didn't stop the bleeding, Jayce might die before he could get to safety or someone found him.

She tried her radio. The shot to her chest had somehow damaged it. Or was that the mud or water? Whatever the case, it wasn't working. Her cell was on the sinking boat along with her Glock. It was more likely one of the men took it as their own. She had no weapon, no means of communication, a bleeding partner and no way out without putting more people in danger. As a deputy, she was a complete and utter failure.

Worst of all, this situation was completely her fault. Jayce was injured and they were both in mortal danger because of her decision to press on. Jayce had wanted to turn back as the day waned. Why hadn't she listened?

Shouts drew her attention. Her heart rate jacked even higher.

They had left the boats and were hunting her.

Be safe, Jayce...

The tree canopy was thick, making the woods dark and eerie. Fury and a lot of fear pushed her from the trunk and she ran deeper into the thick temperate rain forest. The scent of pine and mossy earth enveloped her. She pushed off tree trunks as she trekked, propelling herself onward, and climbed over boulders, making her way up the mountain.

Daylight waned, and she'd soon run out of light.

Bree paused to catch her breath. Had she lost the men yet? She couldn't take a chance and had to keep pushing to make her way to safety.

If she kept close to the river and followed it west, she would eventually find a town. But the way it twisted and turned through the mountains, that would take her twice as long as a straighter path toward Coldwater Bay.

What did she know? She knew the river, that's what. Not the woods.

If only she could wait here for rescuers, but men were hunting her. That was out of the question.

She stumbled on a root and fell. Pain ignited, spreading through her ankle.

"Well, that's just great," she whispered. She wished she could shout, but she knew better than to give herself away.

She pushed to stand on it. Once again, pain knifed through her. She collapsed. Really?

Could things get any worse?

Bree let the tears come. The fear and the tears.

Either the men would locate and kill her, or she would die before she could make it out. No one would find her before it was too late. All that determination she thought she had crumbled as if detonated.

If those men knew how to track, then it wouldn't be long before they found her. But she didn't have to make it easy for them.

She pushed herself into a tree hollow. Brought her knees to her chest. Temporarily safe, she let the tears flow again and thought about her small family. Dad would be worried. He knew her job often kept her late, but she would never miss Stevie's birthday party. At the very least, she would let him know what was going on if she was going to be late.

Oh, God, please let me make it out of this alive, for Stevie's sake! He can't lose someone else. Please help Jayce make it back to his family.

Bree's sister-in-law, Stevie's mom Narelle, had died in a car accident before he'd even turned a year old. That had nearly crushed them all, and she and Dad had rallied around the child and her brother, Steve.

But she would always carry a measure of guilt for the way Steve had died three years ago. She had been on duty that day. Her first week in the marine division. She'd been the one to encourage Steve to enjoy a day on the lake. She was the first one to come upon the accident and find that her brother had drowned.

She let that image run through her now, play-by-play. Quinn Strand—her brother's best friend—holding Steve in his arms.

She didn't blame Quinn but she would always associate him with her brother's death. So even if she still had some unresolved feelings for him, nothing could come of them now. It would all have to stay in the past, where it belonged.

She'd dated the guy in high school—secretly, because Steve had always warned away all her boyfriends. She'd had a serious crush on him then. She'd hoped he had feelings for her, too, that they were working toward something, but then after graduation, Quinn had just disappeared. She'd heard he'd joined the service. Then he'd come back to Coldwater Bay one summer after he'd discharged. Things between them had picked up where they'd left off. He'd been gone far too long, and she'd missed him. He was someone she thought she could fall for.

He'd been driving the boat when the tragedy occurred. Though it had been considered an accident and he hadn't been held negligent, every time she thought of Quinn it reminded her of Steve's death.

Afterward, he left again.

Even if she could forget that he was part of the accident that killed Steve, he was the guy who left her twice without so much as a goodbye. Without so much as an "It's me, not you, Bree."

If only he wasn't the only guy who made her heart pound. Even if someone else could, she wasn't willing to subject herself to the risk of being left again. She'd put that idea, the dream of raising Stevie with a husband, having more children, far from her.

There had to be something truly wrong with her for Quinn to leave her like that. She wasn't worth fighting for. Not worth loving.

So she'd put everything into loving Stevie and making the best family she could for him.

But if Stevie lost Bree tonight, then what?

God, do You hear me? Stevie needs me.

Exhaustion overwhelmed her, and she let herself doze off. Might as well rest while she could. Maybe she would have enough fortitude to push through the pain of her ankle after she rested.

Bree woke up to complete darkness.

Darkness and voices that echoed off the trees.

Quiet footfalls closed in.

They'd found her. Terror threatened to take her survival instincts away, but she steeled her resolve. She would fight them if they found her. If she could just outlast them...

Whoever approached was close. Too close.

She gripped a rock.

Someone reached in and took her arm, his hands strong. Without effort, he pulled her from her hiding place and pressed her back against the tree. Bree smashed the rock into his head. He groaned and fell, dragging her down with him. She had to crawl over him to get away. He grabbed her arm and refused to let go.

"Wait. Bree..."

He knew her name? Something about the voice. She hesitated, then turned back. Moonlight dappled the forest enough for her to see his face.

"Quinn?"

Quinn Strand grabbed his throbbing head. She'd hit him hard. Good for her. She'd thought he was one of the men after her, and if he had been, she wouldn't have succeeded in incapacitating him with the rock. Not so good for her. He composed himself and forced his legs to work.

Easing closer, he kept his voice low and said, "Keep quiet. They're close."

"What are you doing here?" she whispered.

She didn't understand that he'd meant complete silence.

He gripped the thermal imaging monocular he'd used to find her, then sat up. He tucked his hand around her neck and pulled her close so that his cheek was against hers as he whispered in her ear. "They aren't far. Don't talk." He hoped the noise of their scuffle hadn't already alerted them, but there was nothing he could do about it now. He'd explain everything later. "Now hold my hand and stay with me. I'll lead you to safety."

He hoped.

Thankfully, the men after her didn't have a thermal imaging device or else they would have already gutted her and thrown her body in the river. He knew these men. Knew their brutality. He'd bury his regret for leading them across Bree's path for later.

He squeezed her hand, letting her know he was ready. He'd have to move slower with her. It might even be easier to carry her. With thermal imaging he could see the men's heat signatures—much better than night vision, which wouldn't give him the men's locations behind trees or hiding in bushes.

Heat signatures of four men were closing in. Fifteen yards out. Wait. Make that five men. They'd tracked her this far and from his experience, Quinn knew they were like a mixed breed of bloodhound and bulldog—they would never give up until they found her. And once they did, they would never let go.

No way could Quinn leave her at their mercy. He had hoped he could sneak through their ever-tightening circle to get her out, but it would be close. It was a risk to him—but what did he care about the risk to him if Bree got hurt?

She had no idea what she had always meant to him. No idea that he'd carried her picture with him at all times, even when he'd served in a foreign country fighting against a terrorist-producing regime. So many lonely days and nights, he'd pull out the photograph of Bree and just take in her shiny red hair and her bright, compassionate smile. Those brilliant green eyes. That picture had kept him going, even though he'd had no intention of coming back to her. Or for her.

Of making a family with her.

He couldn't afford to grow close to anyone or love them. He couldn't risk the pain of losing someone he loved again.

He'd walked out on her already. Staying away from her was supposed to keep her safe. But still, at this moment, she was in danger of losing her life.

Because of him!

She collapsed behind him and he knelt beside her. Whispered in her ear. "Are you okay?"

"I sprained my ankle."

Without speaking another word, he lifted her in his arms, tucked against his chest. Easier to carry her in a fireman's carry, but this way was more comfortable for her. She might have protested except they were desperate to escape as soundlessly as possible. Quinn knew she understood the danger they faced. She had fought them and lost, though at least she'd held on to her life for a while longer.

Long enough for Quinn to find her and get her out of this.

Holding Bree in his arms under any circumstances wasn't optimal for him. He didn't want to stir up old longings or the buried emotions he had for her. He needed to stay focused on the mission only.

Working as an undercover agent for the DEA—Drug
Enforcement Administration—he'd learned how to kill
his emotions, and he tried to kill those feelings stirring
for Bree right now.

The only thing that mattered was getting her out of
this alive. He wouldn't be able to live with the guilt if
this ended in her death. Especially since she wouldn't
be in this predicament if it weren't for him.

If only he hadn't come back to the Coldwater Bay
area when he'd been forced to run and hide. But he'd
made the mistake of leaving a piece of himself here at
home, and that piece had called to him when he was
in trouble.

He slowed to catch his breath and take in the scen-
ery forming in front of him.

Not a hundred yards ahead, two human heat signatures closed in. Headed for each other. Confabbing? Of
course they would regroup, but then which direction
would they head? He lowered Bree to the ground next
to a tree. His muscles were corded as tight as they'd ever
been, and he hoped she sensed the urgency to keep absolutely quiet. No whispering in his ear.

He eased back into a position to fight and defend.

Prepared to take the men on if he and Bree were
discovered.

The men separated. One walked away, but the other
headed toward the spot where Quinn and Bree were
hiding. The man was no doubt wearing night-vision
goggles and had caught a glimpse of something he intended to investigate. He would find them in moments.
He must have communicated to his buddies since they
were forming a circle too tight for Quinn to go anywhere but straight through the man headed his way.

He backed behind a tree and waited. If necessary, he

would take the man out, but it would have to be done in complete silence or he would draw the rest of them.

He couldn't protect Bree against five armed murderous and brutal drug runners.

TWO

An eerie silence weighed down the forest, the tension prickling through the air and cutting off her breath. She waited in the darkness, understanding that any moment could be her last. She must remain perfectly still. Her lungs ached for oxygen.

Life required breathing, but in this circumstance, breathing where others might hear it could mean death.

She was being hunted.

But with her sprained ankle, she wasn't going very far. She couldn't outrun anyone who might pursue her.

More than that, her head was still spinning, struggling with all of it, but especially the part where her old flame— the man she never wanted to see again—had shown up and rescued her.

She couldn't make out much, but she felt the taut muscle of his arm next to her as they pressed against the scratchy bark of the thick-trunked pine. Felt the heat coming off him. Sensed the tension rolling through him, and that scared her all the more. If Quinn—an ex-marine—was this on edge, then she had every reason to be terrified. With a bum ankle, she could do no rescuing for either of them. Their survival depended on his ability to get them to safety.

While she hoped he was able to succeed, when they were on the other side of danger, he'd better have a good explanation as to why he was here in the wilderness in the middle of her lethal predicament in the first place. She couldn't *wait* to hear why he'd just shown up out of the blue.

With that thought, she listened good and long for a search helicopter. Even if, like her, Jayce hadn't been able to contact anyone to explain what happened, she had hoped that by now someone in the department would have figured out things had gone very wrong and sent a search team. They should be looking for her and Jayce.

In that case, she and Quinn would get their ultimate rescue.

Except she didn't hear a helicopter.

Squeezing her eyes shut, she tried to imagine what could have happened to prevent search crews from combing the woods. Why she didn't hear helicopter blades whooshing above her.

In her gut, she already knew.

She'd contacted Dispatch to let them know of her status and that she and Jayce would be returning with the three men who were transporting some big illegal guns. But that had only been a few hours ago. Maybe they hadn't even organized a search team yet. Dispatch would want to check on her status and when she didn't respond, they would know. Still, disappointment wrapped around her heart and squeezed.

Even when they finally scoured the area looking for their deputies, the sinking of her boat meant searchers wouldn't know where to start unless Jayce had survived and was able to communicate with them.

God, please let him survive! Let him get help!

Quinn leaned close. "Stay here."

Right. Where would she go?

Carefully, she released a heavy sigh and thought maybe her heart went with it. Depending on where they started a search for the lost deputies, the river was over two hundred miles long. They wouldn't immediately think to search for her in the wilderness unless Jayce told them that was where she'd gone.

They wouldn't run into those men on the river. No, those men were searching for Bree. Had probably found a way to hide their boats.

Footfalls let her know someone hiked toward her. Instinctively, she knew it wasn't Quinn. The cadence was off. The breaths came too heavy. Nope. Not Quinn.

She wished she could see better in the dark. Moonlight broke through the canopy and the clouds infrequently. She pressed her body hard against the tree, and tried to calm her breaths. But fear took hold.

If they had night-vision or thermal imaging devices like Quinn's, they would see her before she saw them.

Someone was coming to kill her.

Leaves rustled as someone moved past her. A soft grunt mere feet away kept her frozen in place.

Quinn was suddenly next to her again. She sensed him before she smelled his woodsy scent. His lips were against her ear. "I knocked out one of their men. They're closing in. We have a narrow space and short window in which to escape."

Then he pressed a weapon into her palm. He gathered her into his arms again, careful not to hurt her ankle. Then she held on to his muscular form. Buried her face in his shoulder to breathe in his strength.

She hated being so weak. She was a deputy.

So was Jayce. Was he still alive, or had he died out

here? She'd given him a fighting chance by drawing the men away from him and after her, but had it been enough?

She thought of his wife, Cindy, and baby, Taylor.

Lord, please, help him. Help us!

And poor Stevie, if Bree didn't make it out alive. She didn't want to even think about her father, who had already lost a son. Tears burned her throat, but she held them at bay. Couldn't cry in front of Quinn—though at this moment it wasn't likely he'd notice. But she couldn't risk making a sound. It amazed her that Quinn could tread so quietly while moving quickly and stealthily through that "window" he spoke of.

She tightened her grip on the weapon, a gift, and hoped she wouldn't have to use it, though she was grateful he hadn't left her unarmed.

His breathing increased with his movements through the woods, as she would expect. It felt like the worst sort of ride at an amusement park. Then he suddenly ducked with her. She contained a yelp. What was he seeing? If only she could see, too.

He grunted and fell, dropping her completely. She rolled to sit and scoot out of the way of danger though she didn't know where it would come from. She could only think of one reason he'd fallen as she held the weapon out ready to fire. But she didn't want to accidentally shoot Quinn.

In the darkness, she could barely make out his form struggling with another man.

Between them, a long knife.

Quinn held his arm against the man's throat, choking off his ability to cry for help. But the thug…he got the better of Quinn. How had that happened? He lifted the knife and in a flash would stab Quinn if she didn't stop him.

If she fired the gun, she would alert the others. But Bree had no choice. She had to save Quinn's life. Before she lost her chance, she fingered the trigger and pulled. Gunfire shattered the quiet forest.

The man dropped onto the pine needles.

Shouts ignited the air.

Quinn leaned over the man. "He's dead."

Then he huffed as he marched over to her. "You didn't have to do that. I could have taken him."

"It didn't look that way to me. I'm sorry."

He picked her up, positioned her on his back to ride piggyback and ran for it. She should have thought of this position sooner. It would have been easier for him, though she had to admit, she hadn't exactly hated being in his arms.

"I hope you still have the advantage of seeing them," she whispered.

He didn't respond. He'd have to speak too loudly. But his footfalls were no longer quiet. No longer stealthy.

And that couldn't be good.

God, please help us get to safety. Please help the sheriff, the searchers, find us.

Although…she had the strange feeling that Quinn didn't want to be found.

He ran with everything in him. Pushed harder than he'd ever done before—even on foreign soil. This was Bree. He had to save her.

And just how could Quinn have found himself in this situation with Bree? He pushed the thought away, knowing that the question would only distract him. Time enough for that later.

He forced his thoughts to the mission at hand and concentrated on making it through that window. That hole that had opened up for them—two men on the left side marching toward them. One on the right side. Those men would be jogging if it weren't for the tangle of vines and slick mossy roots and boulders in their path. Quinn was surprised they didn't simply mow everything down with the machine guns.

But he knew why—they might have tried to kill her on the river, but now they wanted to torture her for information and then kill her. Add to that, she'd taken out one of their men tonight, too. Unfortunately, she had also given their position away.

The men probably weren't aware that it was Quinn—the man they were after and the reason they had initially come up the river—helping Bree escape them. At least not yet.

A twig snapped. Much too close.

They were quickly moving in, and Quinn and Bree's opportunity for escape was closing up like some portal from a science fiction movie.

Bree held on tightly. If her arms were wrapped around him any tighter, squeezed any harder—her fingers jamming through his shirt and into his skin—he might struggle to breathe. He wouldn't cry out in pain, though. He'd endured much worse than fingernail stab wounds from a slight and beautiful red-haired, green-eyed deputy.

His heart beat even faster with the thought.

Concentrate, man!

He needed tunnel vision. He forced his thoughts into a laser focus. Thought about nothing but the mission. Nothing but pushing through that space between the glowing bad guys. Quinn let his military training take over, this escape reminiscent of what he'd already experienced.

Except—wait. Too close. Their pursuers were too close. There was no way he could slip past them unheard. Stopping, he waited behind a huge boulder. Held his breath. He suspected that Bree instinctively understood. He thought she was holding her breath, too.

The ring of three men grew tighter, their determination to capture Bree apparent, and like a specter, the fear of that outcome reached out to grab him and choke him. But as they continued to search, they closed their circle in the wrong direction, leaving Quinn and Bree outside. Free to move. Free to escape.

At least for the moment.

He would take advantage and press on, keep moving quickly to put as much distance between them as he could.

Unfortunately, he'd have to go far and wide to lead the men in the wrong direction for when they tried to track him. He had to lead them away from his hidden camp in the thickest part of the woods. Then backtrack. Just the thought of it made him want to groan.

One thing had become painfully clear—despite his best efforts, six months here and he had let himself get out of shape.

"Quinn." Bree's soft voice whispered against his ear unexpectedly, wrapped around him in a way that made his heart skip a beat.

He shook it off.

Man, he'd missed her. He'd missed her every time he left.

"Quinn." Louder now. "You have to stop."

Not yet. He'd keep pushing forward until he dropped. He could keep going forever to save her.

His muscles screamed. His lungs burned.

The past was chasing him down. He couldn't run far enough or fast enough.

And now Bree was caught in the middle.

She struggled against his back, trying to scramble down. Maybe she'd been hurt and he was being a brute not listening to her pleas to stop. He slowed, sucked in air like he couldn't get enough. Eased her off his back.

"Bree—" *gasp, gasp* "—are you—" *gasp* "—okay?"

He bent over his thighs. Just. Couldn't. Get enough air…

"Are you trying to kill yourself?" she asked softly.

"No." He peered through the monocular again for heat signatures. He saw none he'd attribute to humans. Only wildlife.

But that didn't mean they weren't closing in.

He waited until his breathing calmed. "Just trying to…get you…to safety."

She pressed her palms against his cheeks. Close. Too close. "Thank you. I'd be dead right now if it weren't for you. But don't give yourself a heart attack on my account."

He put his hand against hers on his cheek, then stepped back. He didn't need her getting so close. "I'm not going to have a heart attack. Don't worry. But getting you to safety is my responsibility now."

"I don't know how or why, but you rescued me. Those men are after me and now they're after you, too. I'm sorry for that."

"You're wrong."

It's my fault. All my fault…

But now wasn't the time to tell her.

A branch cracked. He stilled. Could be trees clacking in the light breeze.

Or someone closing in that he couldn't see yet. If that was the case, then he'd rested too long.

Though he didn't want to lean in close enough to feel her warmth, he did it anyway. "Time to go."

"Are you sure?"

"I can go a hundred miles." But he hoped he wouldn't have to.

Without saying more, she climbed onto his back again. Trusting him? Nah. He had never given her a reason to trust him. In fact, if anything he'd proven to her that she *couldn't* trust him.

At least with her heart.

Nor did he trust *himself* with her heart.

THREE

This night was turning into pure torture. She couldn't do this anymore. After holding tight to Quinn's back, locked in one position with no opportunity to shift or reposition, her body ached as if she'd been riding a horse for hours. She couldn't see where they were going and feared at any moment a bullet would burrow into her back. She knew that Quinn tried to be careful, but small branches slapped her cheeks and arms from time to time. She kept her eyes closed to protect them, but there was nothing much she could do for the rest of her. And bugs—she had to have acquired a spider or beetle or two during their trek. Just the thought of creepy-crawlers had goose bumps rising on her flesh.

Of course, Quinn was going through far worse. So how did she explain that she needed to rest? Their lives were far more important than her need to ease her aches and pains.

Except she simply couldn't hold on anymore.

As if reading her mind, Quinn slowed down, then stopped and nearly stumbled. He leaned over to allow her to slip off. She stepped on her ankle then fell. He caught her before she hit the ground and held her steady.

"Are you okay?"

"I forgot about my ankle. I'm good." She reached for the nearest tree trunk to prop herself against. She could stand with something to lean on as long as she didn't use her injured ankle. The pain had been forgotten, but the throbbing came back strong now. She stretched her back and arms, surprised at how stiff she was.

Then she took in their surroundings. She thought Quinn had stopped from sheer exhaustion, but now it appeared there was more to it. The trees were thick around them but in this spot, they had thinned out, allowing moonlight through in the moments when fast-moving clouds weren't drifting by. Vines and ferns grew up and around what she thought might be a structure against the side of an incline. A ridge, maybe.

It was beautiful. Like some kind of fairyland. She must be beyond exhausted to be thinking like that now.

"What is this place?" she asked.

"It's my home. At least, it has been for the last six months."

"Oh." *Wow.* "Isn't this a wilderness area?" As a deputy who worked near national parks in the county, she understood that a wilderness area was federally owned land, meant to remain undeveloped without structures or improvements or habitation. Hmm.

"Don't worry. We're right on the edge of the wilderness, but this is private property—it's a friend's deer lease. He hunts here during deer hunting season. It's about as far as you can get from civilization with a camper."

Oh, now she saw it. A camper was hidden beneath the vines and greenery—well, silvery in the moonlight. "How did he get this camper up here? There aren't even any roads."

"None that you can easily see. That's why I like it."

Quinn glanced through the woods. "Let's take this conversation inside. Get fueled, hydrated and rested. I don't know how long we have."

Quinn assisted her forward, moving vines out of the way until she could make out an actual door. Then she recognized the camper as a small Casita travel trailer. He'd lived here for the last six months?

She definitely wanted to know why.

Inside the camper, he turned on a light, dimming it enough that it would be imperceptible from outside. Electricity and water would be an issue up here but obviously Quinn had that all figured out.

Something crawled over her arm. She yelped and slapped her arm free of the insect.

She glanced around the small space—were they any spiders or rodents?—and rubbed her tired arms. The place was much neater than she would have expected of a guy living alone.

He busied himself at the small kitchen. "I know what you're thinking."

"Oh yeah? What's that?"

"You were expecting the place to be trashed out."

Yeah, well, she'd known him as a teenager. He was no different from her brother... Oh. She wished she hadn't thought of Steve, because it brought that same image to mind—Quinn holding her dead brother, his friend. The utter remorse on his face. Tears surged in her eyes. And for the first time, she thought about Quinn's expression as he carried Steve, the devastation *he* must have felt. Bree had only ever been concerned about Dad and Stevie, and her own loss. Somehow, that now seemed selfish of her.

She pushed the image far from her and tried to calm her nerves. Her muscles ached and she needed to rest—

but like Quinn said, they didn't know how long they had. If those men tracked them here, then they'd have to run again.

She wanted to believe that they'd stop looking, but a persistent sense of unease told her she wasn't safe. Not yet. Bree couldn't fathom what had happened on the river, or this night of running. Who would have thought they would try so hard to kill her?

Give it up already.

She was so exhausted, all she could think about was closing her eyes, and she hadn't been the one trekking through the woods with the weight of another person on his back for half the night.

She eyed the small bed on the far side—where Quinn would sleep. She was fine with the sofa on this side. But wait. What was she thinking? She wasn't going to stay long enough for that. Bree could sleep for a thousand years, but not until she was safe at home and Stevie was in her arms. And Dad knew that she was all right.

Now. How did she get there?

Bree realized Quinn was waiting for her to reply to his comment about her expecting the place to be a mess. "Oh, yeah, I was, actually. You were really sloppy."

"These days, I have to keep it perfectly clean or I'd go crazy. I couldn't function. Plus, I need to be able to flee at any moment and don't want to have to search for stuff."

Flee at any moment? Now that got her attention. She sat up and blinked, hoping she could keep her eyes open.

What was going on? She wanted answers from Quinn, but first she had some explaining to do herself.

He handed her a tall glass of water he must haul up here in plastic jugs. How else could he get it?

As she drank, he guzzled down his own and watched her over the rim of his glass. His blue-gray eyes stared at her. Eyes she used to look into all dreamily. That was before reality hit her hard—Quinn would leave her again. And again.

She still couldn't get over the fact that Quinn had rescued her. She could remember the moment of surprise mixed with relief at seeing a friendly face, then with anger all over again, the way she always felt around him these days, at the way he'd left her—with a dead brother to remember him by. And yet now that he was here, her heart warmed to see him—she'd missed him so much. At the same time, she had never wanted to see him again.

She had mixed emotions when it came to this man—no doubt there.

But none of their past mattered while they were in danger. She finished the last of her water. She hadn't realized how thirsty she was.

"I'm so sorry for dragging you into this, Quinn. But…how did you find me? What are you even doing here?"

He slowly set the glass on the counter and scraped both hands through his thick, shaggy hair. Her heart jumped around inside—she had always been so attracted to him, and unfortunately, now wasn't any different. Angry with herself, she pushed from the sofa though she was a little unsteady on her feet, especially her injured ankle. She leaned against the counter to support her weight.

"What's going on, Quinn?" She tried to read his somber expression.

He leveled his gaze on her. *Oh no. Here it comes.* She wasn't so sure she wanted to know.

"You didn't drag me into this." Hands on his hips, he turned his back on her.

"Quinn."

A few seconds passed, then, "It's my fault that you're in the middle."

"Start talking."

When he turned, she thought she might have seen him hiding a grin. "You were never the patient kind."

"Quinn!"

He held his hands in the air and pressed his palms down. "Keep your voice down. We don't want to lead anyone here."

She eased forward but not too close. Maybe if she backed off the pressure, he would talk. She recalled easily enough that pressure was the wrong tactic with him. He would run rather than face it.

He took several long breaths. "Those men you ran into—they came here looking for me. I... I've been dreading this day. Hoping it would never happen, but keeping an eye out for it, all the same. From my perch here, if I look just so, I can view the river. I saw the whole thing from the moment you and your partner pulled up alongside them. I was watching it through my binoculars. I never prayed so hard, Bree. Well, there was one other time..."

Yeah, she knew exactly what time that was. He had prayed hard for Steve to live.

She said nothing, though, waiting for him to continue.

"As soon as I saw you go into the water, I followed you and saw you swim away. I started making my way down. It was dark by the time I found you, but I had my monocular so I kept searching and praying I could find you. There was only one real path you could have taken with the way the ravine twists along the river, and unfortunately, only one path the men after you could have taken."

"Well, even if they came here for you, they're after me now, too. But I have to ask—who are they and why are they searching for you?"

"Anything I tell you could put you in more danger." She huffed.

"You seem a little indignant."

"You think? Seriously, Quinn, I'm already in danger. Jayce McBride, my partner and a good deputy, a husband and a father—he's in danger. He made it out of the water, but I have no idea if he crawled on the bank to die or if he has been rescued...or if he's still out there, trying to evade capture. Now, after everything I've just been through, I deserve to know, especially if what you say is true—that those men were on the river looking for you. Are you going to tell me?"

He hung his head. "I'm so sorry about everything." He sucked in a long breath, then, "I was working undercover and they found out. That's a betrayal they won't easily forget, so they hunted me all the way here from Louisiana."

Bree's heart twisted in a hundred directions. She sucked in a breath. "Who are you working with?"

"DEA..."

Drug Enforcement Administration.

"Was, anyway."

Obviously, there was much more to it.

Favoring her good leg, she tightened the belt on her uniform pants. She'd lost her own weapon. Her radio wasn't working. But that didn't change a thing. "I'm Deputy Carrington, Quinn, and if you're being threat-

ened then it's my job to protect you. Let's get you back
to civilization and I can put you in protective custody."

He swallowed the laugh that almost erupted.
Not going to happen.
Aww, Bree... Look at you.
He took in her messy, muddy face and hair—he
couldn't even tell if it was red now—and the scratch
along her cheek. She probably got that from their wild
run through the forest. That needed cleaning. He re-
sisted the urge to cup her face. Wished he could take
the pain of this night away.

The truth was that all Quinn would ever be to Bree
was a pain-maker. But he could at least address the
smallish pains. "Wait here."

"Where are you going?"

"Just grabbing a first aid kit." He didn't have far to go
in the small space, and was soon wiping away the mud
from her cheek, then cleaning the scratch. "Let's take
care of these nicks and cuts before we head out again."

"Thanks, but Quinn, you're avoiding responding to
my offer."

In her eyes, he saw that he'd hurt her by not taking
her up on her promise of protection. But it was ridiculous at best. She had no idea what she was committing
to. No idea that she was only getting herself in deeper
with her offer to help—that is, if he were to take her
up on it.

He searched inside the kit, then hung his head. "I
never meant to drag you or anyone else into this. I was
hiding where no one could find me and yet I led them
right into your path."

"And just how did they find you?"

"That's something I'd like to know as well, but it's

a question for another day. Right now, I need to wrap that ankle. Attend to the other scratches." Get a rag to wipe away the mud from her face and hair. She could really use some clean clothes, as could he.

Her eyes were kind of glazing over now. "Sit down, Bree."

Oddly, she allowed him to guide her to the sofa. He frowned. Was she going into shock? "Bree, tell me this."

"What?"

"I know you've worked as a deputy for a few years. Have you ever killed anyone in the line of duty before?"

She studied her shaky hands and shook her head. "No. I… I've never exchanged gunfire like that. Nor had Jayce. The movies make it look like we do that all the time, but…"

"I know." He knew, all right. He remembered the first person he'd taken out in the line of duty—first, as a soldier overseas. And then, unfortunately, in his job with the DEA. It had changed him. He didn't like it.

He squeezed her shoulder. "It's okay. Take your time." She would need a lot of time to process that she'd shot and killed one of the bad guys tonight, even though she was a trained deputy. She was still human, after all, and taking a life would affect her in every way—spiritually, psychologically and mentally.

He sucked in a breath. He'd done this to her, too, put her in a situation where she'd had to take a life. Eventually, she might have been forced to take someone out in her job as a deputy. But maybe not. He couldn't be sure. And anyway, the fact that she'd had to do so tonight was on him.

He had to get her back to civilization. She needed care and counseling.

Quinn was beyond care and counseling—and his

only concern in this life was one thing: getting Bree
to safety.

He lifted her chin to look into her beautiful green
eyes—sad, grief-stricken eyes. They stabbed his heart,
broke it open. She wanted to cry. He could see her eyes
shimmering with emotion.

Quinn wanted to draw her into his arms and comfort
her. Make the bad men go away. If only they lived in a
world where they could be together and Quinn wouldn't
bring her harm or pain, and hey, as long as he was wishing, why not wish for Steve to be alive, too?

She blinked and moved away from his touch. In her
eyes, her expression, he saw the same fire and determination he knew he'd eventually find there—it stirred
back to life. Good. That was much better than seeing
her defeated.

The last time he'd seen Bree in Coldwater Bay and
looked in her eyes, he'd been holding her brother Steve's
body. His best friend. The man had drowned in a boat-
ing accident. Quinn had been on the boat with him.
Though he hadn't been charged, he'd held himself responsible, and so had Bree, he was sure. She hadn't said
as much, but he knew. He'd taken one look in her eyes
then and seen the massive hurt and utter disappointment. It had cut him to the soul.

After being the sole survivor of the car accident that
had killed his parents when he was a teenager, what
had he been thinking to believe he could ever be close
to or love someone? It would all turn to death and ash.
That's why he'd taken off again, even leaving his sisters behind.

But he'd tried. Oh, he'd tried with Bree. The second
time he tried—after he'd returned from his military
service—he'd actually let himself love her. Then her

brother had drowned. Quinn had known at that moment that he didn't deserve to love or to live a life filled with love. He'd been too afraid that even if he tried, tragedy would strike again. And now it appeared he definitely brought that death and danger with him.

He'd thought he could never look in her eyes again. So he'd left. He'd found the darkest place, a place he knew he would never be tempted to love, and he'd joined the DEA to fight another kind of war—the drug war.

The evil he'd experienced there made him feel dirty. Soiled. He wanted to wipe himself clean but he couldn't get away. The darkness, the evil had followed him here to hurt Bree.

What had he been thinking to come back to Cold-water Bay?

His dangerous and dark job had gotten the best of him. And suddenly, the question burned and he had to know the answer. "You do believe me about why the men are after me, don't you?"

"I want to, Quinn. But why not go to your superiors? Why not tell someone in the DEA—they could protect you."

"Because someone on the inside is dirty. I don't know everyone involved and I have to know who I can trust first. I was trying to find that out when my cover was suddenly blown and the leader of the group I infiltrated sent hitmen to kill me." He squeezed his eyes shut. He didn't want to imagine what those men would do to Bree if they got to her.

Because of him.

Why, God?

"So you just left your job?"

He nodded. "I'm hiding from the good guys and the bad guys. I can't tell which is which."

She frowned. "So you, what—just thought you could hide here forever?"

Not forever. "I just had to get away. Let things die down. Figure out who I could trust. I shouldn't have come anywhere near Coldwater Bay. But I didn't know where to go. I knew I couldn't go running back to Aunt Debby or bring danger to my family. But I ended up near home anyway." He'd thought he was discreet enough, hiding out in the wilderness, not contacting his family. But on his supply runs in town, he would spend time at an internet café and search for information, anything to help. Maybe that had been too risky, and he'd been located because of his activities.

"I guess something about Coldwater Bay just drew you back." A smile from her?

That surprised him.

"I guess so. I never meant to bring danger to you." Despite his efforts to stay away, he found himself looking in her eyes again, and her gaze swept his heart up into her current. "Bree—" What? What could he possibly say to make it all better? "We should be safe here for a few hours at least. You don't need to try to protect me. You can't put me into protective custody. That wouldn't be a good idea for either of us. I'll get you to safety and then I need to disappear again."

He wouldn't think his words, his promise to disappear, would surprise her. After all, he'd done just that at least twice with her. But her jaw hung open while she processed his words.

"If anyone asks," he continued, "you never saw me. Do you understand?"

A loud *snap* resounded.

Someone had just triggered one of Quinn's booby traps.

FOUR

"What was that?" Bree asked.

Quinn pressed a finger to his lips.

Bree held perfectly still. Quinn's reaction could mean only one thing—the men had somehow found them.

She fought the overwhelming urge to hyperventilate. Hadn't she just ridden half the night on Quinn's back to escape?

Quinn moved like a predatory big cat, making no sound in pursuit of his prey. And that was just it—*he* was being hunted. They were being hunted together now. But his actions made it appear that he was the one doing the hunting. Maybe he could end this and they could stop running and call for help.

Her eyes darted around the camper. Did he have a communication device here? A cell or a satphone? She didn't spot anything, nor could she bring herself to get up and search. At the moment, fear had paralyzed her. Come to think of it, it was probably safer not to stand, anyway. If she knew what was good for her, she would drop to the floor. Quietly, of course. Those men could spray this camper with bullets—demolish it completely.

A moment later, Quinn snuffed out the small lamp and utter darkness engulfed her.

Quinn! She wanted to call his name but feared making the slightest sound. A cool draft hit her. Goose bumps crawled over her.

And just like that…she knew she was alone inside the camper.

No warmth emanated from another body. No slight intake of breath. None of that sensation of another presence. Just the slightest shift in the air, the atmosphere.

How had he escaped the camper without her knowing? Through another opening besides the door? And he'd just left her here? She shouldn't be so surprised.

She fisted her hands. Held back her anger and disappointment. She should be relieved he could enter and exit that quietly. That he had prepared for just this situation and had it all figured out. And why not? He'd been here long enough to plan for this moment. All that time, without reaching out or letting any of the people who cared about him know he was here.

As for her, she hadn't expected any of this so couldn't have planned for it. Like the rushing river that had tried to take her down and under and carry her away, she'd been out of control, and had to force her way up for breath. Had to make her way to the riverbank. She felt completely out of her depth here, but she was determined to force her way out of this. She had a family waiting for her on the other side of the wilderness and unlike some people, she would do everything in her power to go home to the people she loved. That meant standing up and taking action.

Right now.

He could need her help. He'd needed it before, despite his denial.

Okay. That was it. She would find a way on her own out of this camper before it turned into a death trap.

He might be furious; then again, he might very well thank her.

God, a little help, please? Stevie, he needs me. You know he does. If something happens to me, then Dad will be devastated, too. Help me find a way out of here. Help me to help Quinn.

A *thump* sounded somewhere in the camper. Wait. *Inside* the camper? She must be mistaken. Unless…

"Quinn?" she whispered.

No. She had to get out now! Forget about finding Quinn's trapdoor.

Bree fled in the direction of the main door, gritting her teeth through the throb in her ankle.

I can make it. I have to make it.

This was life-and-death. She didn't have time to take it slow and keep quiet. She grappled with the doorknob— any moment someone could grab her from behind. Finally, she threw it open and fled the camper.

She stumbled down the short steps and nearly fell but caught herself, holding back the ridiculous whimper lodged in her throat, from both pain and fear.

Behind her, the door slammed shut.

Good job, Bree.

She had certainly given away that there was a camper if anyone was clueless. But someone had been inside and possibly searching for a warm body in the darkness so they could wrap their hands around a throat. Even though she didn't know what she'd be facing out here, it felt better to be out than in.

She calmed her breathing. Her rapid heart rate. She could see better out here and protect herself. At least she still had the gun Quinn had given her. With trembling limbs, she remained behind a thick tangle of vines that loosely fell over the trailer and waited for whoever might come for her. Why, oh, why did she have to sprain her ankle?

Where are you, Quinn?

She had training in self-defense and law enforcement moves, but she didn't have Quinn's military training, which was far superior to anything she knew. She wouldn't kid herself to think she could fight like him. But if she survived this, she would take extra training classes. Suggest it for all the deputies.

Footfalls crunched much too near.

The cadence was off.

Whoever was coming wasn't Quinn. She held the weapon up but couldn't see what or whom she was aiming at. Not good. Even if the footsteps sounded wrong, she couldn't know with 100 percent accuracy it wasn't Quinn.

A flicker of moonlight illuminated the silhouette of a big man as he stepped closer to the camper. It didn't look like he wore night-vision goggles.

Her hands trembled. If she fired the weapon, she would be taking another life. She prayed he wouldn't look at her. Wouldn't somehow know she waited in the shadows.

Don't look. Don't look. Don't make me do it.

The man turned his head in her direction.

Was she breathing too loudly? Were his senses that well-honed? Without entering the camper, the man turned and walked away.

She released a quiet sigh of relief.

Her body was slammed full force against the camper. She fired off a shot, but missed. He ripped the gun from her hand and tossed it aside. Bright lights floated around in her vision. An arm pressed against her throat, lifting her off the ground and pinning her against the Casita.

She kicked and wrestled, all her focus on pulling his arm away from her throat, but it was no use. Pressure built in her head.

I'm going to die! God, help me!

"Got you." The man ground out the words, his hot breath hitting her face.

Maybe she didn't have top military elite forces training, but she could knee the jerk. Lungs burning for air, she had a few short seconds. She kicked him where it hurt him the most and made it count.

He grunted, then dropped her. Her feet hit the ground and her bum ankle gave out. She crumpled beneath him and sucked in air. Forced her limbs into action so she could crawl away and find the weapon he'd discarded. The man grabbed her leg. She turned and kicked him in the face. He growled and reached for her again, and once he had a hold of her, pain ignited with his brutal grip as he made to crawl on top of her.

Quinn appeared out of nowhere.

Again.

He freed her from the man's grip and lifted him. Her attacker was now the one who got to be slammed against the Casita. It probably had a huge dent in it as hard as Quinn had thrown him. She started her search for the gun again. Quinn wasn't carrying one that she could readily see, but he punched the man instead of using a weapon.

The man dropped unconscious to the ground.

Quinn turned to her then and lifted her to stand. He gripped her arms, sounding out of breath. "Are you okay?"

"Yes. But I had it under control." Isn't that what he'd said to her when she had saved him, even though he'd been in denial?

"I'm glad to hear it. I might not be around next time.

It's good to know you can handle yourself against the worst kinds of thugs."

Wait. He thought she was serious. He thought she would have won that fight against that huge, brutal man. Well, she'd go along with it. "I'm a deputy, after all."

"I know."

Who was she kidding? This wasn't the kind of engagement they practiced in law enforcement training. She would be changing her training days once she made it out of this. In the meantime, she wanted answers.

"Where did you go? You just left me there for bait. Was that your plan all along?"

Her accusation was like a brass-knuckled fist to his gut, knocking the breath from him. Leaving him momentarily stunned. He composed himself and inhaled the oxygen she'd kicked out of him. She really had a much lower opinion of him than he'd realized, and that was pretty low to begin with. He ignored the pain creeping across his heart and reached for the man on the ground.

How did he pick him up?

This guy was beefy—all muscle and brawn, and that, combined with his obvious military background, made him a lethal foe. He had to hurry before the guy regained consciousness.

He hadn't really thought she could take him on her own, but she needed reassurance from him that she could do this. He didn't exactly want her waiting around for him to show up. She was a deputy and he believed in her. But when he got the chance, he would teach Bree some invaluable defensive moves, if she'd let him.

He hauled the guy up and over his shoulder to carry him.

"I want an answer, Quinn. Did you leave me there for bait? To draw this guy out?"

He didn't have time to stand around and put her concerns to rest. So he'd work while he talked, though they should keep it quiet. He headed for the camper door.

"How could you even suggest that?" He ground his molars. "Could you get the door, please?"

She limped over and propped it open long enough for him to carry the guy inside. He kept forgetting about that ankle. Too bad about that. They could make much better time if she weren't injured.

Inside the camper in the dark, he made his way to where he knew the sofa to be and dropped the unconscious man, wincing when he heard the *thud*. Had he just broken the sofa or had he missed it completely? Quinn flipped the light switch on.

"What are you doing?" she asked.

He turned on her then. He and Bree—they'd always had sparks, and sometimes not necessarily the good kind. Like the sparks flying now. "First things first. Keep your voice down, please. Secondly, you don't actually think I would leave you here to draw this guy to you, do you?" But he didn't wait for her answer. He wasn't sure he wanted to know. "To be clear, no. Absolutely not. I didn't use you for bait."

"You disappeared and left me here. How did you get out of here, anyway?"

"I have a trapdoor for such occasions."

"That's what I thought. Which brings me back to my point—you left me here alone without telling me the plan."

"For your safety. I thought you understood. I needed to check who or what set off the booby trap. My plan was to confront him myself, not lead him to you. The trap had been triggered but I couldn't see anyone. I... I forgot the thermal imaging monocular." Because being near Bree threw off his equilibrium. He'd better get her to safety and stay far away from her. "Then I heard the gun go off and when I got back you were fighting off this guy outside. So why didn't you stay put?"

"Because...because I thought someone had come into the cabin with me. It was weird. Just like you left undetected, it was as if someone had come inside. I felt a draft and heard something inside."

"What?" Quinn's heart rate ratcheted up. "Are you sure?"

"I don't know. How can I know for sure? I fled the camper. But while I was outside, I hid in the vines and this guy tried to come inside, then thought better of it and walked away. Or so I thought. He only came around behind me to nab me."

"I knew you were in trouble, but why didn't you shoot him when you had the chance?"

"I tried but I missed. I don't know what's the matter with me. I'm not utilizing my law enforcement training. As soon as I saw him, I should have at least told him to freeze and cuffed him."

"You still have your cuffs?"

"No. Jayce had them to cuff the men. But I could have tied the guy up."

He honestly couldn't tell if she was being sarcastic. He was being too hard on her. "Look, I'm sorry. This hasn't exactly been the best day for either of us. I'm sorry I left you alone. I thought you understood to stay put and keep quiet. I should have explained. Next time, I won't expect you to read my mind. Is that better?"

"Yes. Now, what are you doing with him? Torture him for information?"

"There isn't time for that." Had he just winked? He sighed and grabbed some plastic ties. "But I'll tie him up, take his radio, cell and weapons—guns and knives.

His shoes to make it more difficult for him in the woods. Everything but his clothes."

"And you're just going to leave him here?"

"Do you have a better suggestion?"

"We could take him with us."

"No. We can't. I can't carry you and drag him along at the same time. Or even force him to come along. Besides, his friends can't be far behind. They aren't going to stop looking for us. They'll find him soon enough. He could have signaled them already that he found the trailer. So we need to leave now."

Quinn gathered the pack he'd saved for the day he would have to flee and never return. He honestly hadn't believed this day would come. He certainly never imagined Bree would be part of it.

He opened the pack and glanced inside just to be sure he had it all. Hydration. Protein bars. An extra gun and ammo. Dropped in this guy's goods—as much as he could fit inside.

It should be enough for him to get Bree back to civilization. Except…he'd have to carry her *and* the pack. Exhaustion threatened. He'd hoped to stay in the cabin to rest for a bit, but that was no longer an option.

"Okay, just so we're clear. You're riding on my back again. And you'll be wearing this pack."

"What? No, Quinn, that's too much weight for you to carry."

"You weigh, what—a buck twenty? In the military, I carried a 120-pound pack in addition to the gear I wore, so it's not like I haven't done this before." So what if he was out of practice. Served him right.

"No time to argue." He shifted his gaze to take her in. Bree was athletic. Strong. Trained. She would make it. Together, they would make it. Quinn would ensure it if it was the last thing he did. "Are you ready?"

She opened her mouth to argue more, but let it go and nodded.

Quietly, they exited the camper. Quinn led her around to the other side where it backed up onto a ridge. Nobody could easily approach from the back side. Still, he looked at the path ahead with the monocular for signs of danger. Morning would come earlier than he would like and expose them. He preferred the darkness so he could stay hidden himself and could more easily see his enemies before they saw him.

His enemies. Now Bree's enemies, too.

This new development bumped up his timeline to expose the darkness chasing him. He'd waited too long, if these men had found him and come for him, endangering someone he cared about. Both of their lives were in danger now. And more than that, if they made it out of this, their hearts were in danger, too. The last thing he ever wanted to do was hurt Bree again. That would crush him.

The sooner he could get her to safety, the better for them both.

FIVE

She would almost rather be facing off with bad guys in a shoot-out. Almost. Holding on to Quinn as he made his way over treacherous, terrifying landscape was proving to be a rigorous test of her mettle. But if he could pass, then she could, too.

At least she'd keep telling herself that.

Even in the coldest part of a summer night, sweat beaded on Bree's brow. At her temples. Along the middle of her back. And worse—on the palms of her hands. As if mirroring her thoughts, her hands slipped apart, and she grabbed his arms before falling completely away.

"Stop, Quinn. Just stop."

"I can't stop here. Just wait."

"I meant as soon as you can. I'm afraid I'm going to slip off." *And fall to my death.*

He grunted with the effort of slowly making his way down the ridge. Finally, he positioned himself to release her.

She climbed off and shrugged out of his pack. "It's no use."

"You're not giving up already, are you?" he asked.

"I'm not one to give up. But this isn't working. There

has to be something better than mountain climbing our way to safety. Maybe we could just follow the riverbank. We might run into someone with a boat."

He offered her water, which she eagerly took, and after chugging half of it, she angled her head. "You hear that?"

"Yeah. A helicopter."

Her heart skipped a beat.

"They're searching for us." *God, please let them find Jayce.* She hoped they already had. He could tell them where to find her, or at least the direction she'd run.

Her heart sank again as she realized that even if Jayce told them the last place he'd seen her, Quinn had taken them far from where this had all started.

"At night?" he asked.

"Sheriff Garrison won't give up on finding us, even at night." And sitting up high on the ridge and above the thick tree canopy, she could more easily see the hint of graying skies as morning would soon dawn. It would be easier for them to be spotted soon.

"In the meantime, we can't just sit around and wait," he said. "We have to keep going."

"We could somehow signal them. Have you got a flare in that bag?"

"No. And even if I did, your sheriff's department isn't the only one searching." Quinn finally took a seat next to her and rubbed the back of his neck. "We can't afford to draw their attention and bring them down on us. They would kill us before we could be rescued, don't you understand?"

She tried to push down the rising disappointment. How could she signal the good guys and let them know she was here without letting the bad guys know, too?

I'm here. Look, see, I'm here! Despite Quinn's warning, she wanted to jump up and down on the rock. Maybe signal with a flashlight. But she couldn't see the helicopter yet. She could only hear it. She'd wait for that opportunity if it came. Even if her signal alerted the bad guys, at least the searchers would know to rescue them.

Except the sound grew distant until she could no longer hear it.

No...

She and Quinn would have to make it out on their own.

Bree drank more water and studied Quinn. Surreal. Absolutely surreal that she sat next to him now. The reasons why were even more incredible.

"So all this time you've been here hiding—literally, hiding—and you haven't even contacted your sisters?"

He shook his head. "It's not that I didn't want to see them. I haven't been the model brother, I know that. I just...after Mom and Dad died in the accident—" he blew out a breath "—and I survived, I think I struggled to be close to anyone." He lifted his head enough to peer at her from under his brows.

She read him then. *You of all people should know that.*

Yes, she did know. She wished things could have been different for him. If his parents had survived, would things have turned out differently for Bree and Quinn? Would they have gotten married and had kids? Would Steve still be alive? So many what-ifs, it could drive her crazy if she let it. Strange how one event could change so many lives. But none of that mattered. What mattered was this moment in time.

And this hurting person next to her.

She wished there were something she could do or

say to make it all better, but in the end, Quinn had to work through his issues himself. He'd tried, she'd give him that. Serving in the armed forces, and then working with the DEA. And now she realized that he'd tried with her, too. But he couldn't give any more. For all his bravery, his guts and strength, the guy was actually afraid to live. What he was doing now didn't really count as living because, to Bree, without love, what was life?

Quinn was too afraid of losing someone—anyone, be it a wife or a sister—so he couldn't get close or cherish anyone. He couldn't embrace life.

But who was she to judge?

She winced. She wasn't in much better condition herself. Quinn had certainly cured her of her willingness to subject herself to being left behind without so much as an "it's me, not you" breakup.

Except despite her issues with relationships, no one had ever made her heart pound like him. Even now, sitting next to him in this life-and-death situation, she wanted to be in his arms. Her mind immediately jumped to the kisses they'd shared when dating.

She was so pathetic. Time to shift her thoughts.

"I ran into both Jonna and Sadie on the job once," she said, referring to his sisters. "It's been a while."

"Oh yeah?" He finished his water with one long gulp.

He tried to appear nonchalant, but she could see in his eyes that he craved hearing something about his family. Poor Quinn. Really, he made this life for himself, and she shouldn't feel sorry for him, but maybe it was more compassion that she felt. She understood his fear. He'd been damaged as a kid when he lost his parents and had never recovered.

"I don't know if you keep up with them. Call them

or anything. I mean, before, when you weren't hiding. Or if you even showed up at their weddings."

"I knew they got married."

Sad.

He flinched at the disappointed look she gave him and she felt a pang of remorse. She hadn't meant to reveal her thoughts that way.

In return, he tossed her an incredulous scowl. "Hey, don't look at me like that. I was in the middle of a bad situation and I couldn't just flit off to a wedding. Do I regret it? Of course I do. I hated everything about my life then, and, honestly, now. You think I wanted to be holed up here, waiting the bad guys out and hoping for an opportunity to turn things around? But not seeing my sisters get married—sure, it was a high price to pay but that's the cost of the work I did."

"Undercover work?"

He nodded. "You really have no idea how ugly working undercover for the DEA can get, but that's a story for another time."

Another time? Would they see each other again once he helped her get back to town? She doubted it. And if the criminals they were running from were any indication of how bad it could get working undercover in the drug wars, she thought she might understand—at least a little.

"So you ran into them. How were they doing?" The tone in his voice revealed how much he missed them.

If only Bree could help him find his way back to Coldwater Bay for real, without all this hiding business.

"Well, the circumstances in which I saw them weren't the best. I was working. Sadie had a run-in with a bad guy. I was there at the end when we arrested the man responsible and took statements. He was involved in maritime drug running and exotic drug schemes. She met her Coast Guard Investigative Service husband that way, though."

Quinn leaned back on his elbows and drew his face up to the gray morning sky. Closed his eyes as if soaking in her words. She wanted to run her fingers through his hair. Comfort him. But if telling him about his sisters brought him a measure of happiness, she could do that, too.

"And Jonna? What about her?"

"She had come to help protect Sadie. Gage Sessions, the CGIS guy, had called her. She looked good when I saw her. Then, later, she had some bad guys from her past show up at the inn. She and her bodyguard worked that out. Took care of it all. Sorry I don't have more details, but I'm only sharing what I know working for the sheriff's department. I can tell you she married the bodyguard."

"I knew that. I know they live at the lodge on the coast," he said, "but also run a security consulting business."

She smiled. "I'm glad to hear that you do try to keep up with them."

"And Cora, did she run into a bad guy, too?"

"I don't know. I saw in the paper she got married to someone with NCIS."

He grinned then. "All three of them married to protective men. I'm glad to hear it, since I couldn't be there to be the protective brother for them."

She heard the pain in his voice.

"But you *are* a protector, Quinn." She touched his arm, wanting to give so much more comfort. "You're protecting *me*."

* * *

Oh, please don't do that...

Her simple touch on his arm sent a fully charged current through him. She'd been the one woman he'd wanted and thought he could love for a lifetime. But now after everything, even if he decided to allow himself to love her, he didn't deserve her. Not after leaving her. Not after what happened with her brother.

Weird how it took all his willpower to keep his hands anchored to the rocks. Keep his arms from wrapping around her and feeling the warmth coming from her body and pouring from her heart, the emotion he knew she wanted to give.

If only he could give back.

He thought of the Bree he'd known in high school. So full of life and energy. They'd had some of the best times two people who were deeply infatuated with each other—maybe even loved each other—could have. She was naive back then, as he'd been. He risked a glimpse at her sitting on the rock, looking on as the sun rose over the mountains, and he took in the beautiful woman she'd become. It could take his breath away if he let it.

And he absolutely couldn't let it. Had to refocus if he wanted to keep them alive.

He shifted on the rock and stretched. They'd rested long enough.

The sun would soon light up the sky completely, and much too soon. They needed to be far away from their pursuers by then. Once he delivered her to the town and the sheriff where she would be safe, that should be the last time he'd see her. Her law enforcement brothers and sisters would keep her safe. The thought that he wouldn't see her again weighed on his heart heavier than he'd expected.

Still, he let himself smile. To think he was sitting here with Bree watching the sun rise. He went as far as to let himself chuckle. "You're a protector, too, Bree. You probably don't even need me to help you. And if it weren't for the men after me and now you, then you wouldn't have seen me."

"You wouldn't have come to assist me even if it had been some other kind of criminals?" A little hurt crackled through her soft voice.

A lump grew in his throat. Would he have? "Why should I? You're a capable deputy. But I just happened to know how utterly brutal those men are. When I watched them on the river with my binoculars, I couldn't believe it was them. That Michael Jones, the head of the drug gang in the New Orleans area, had actually sent them. I recognized one of his hit men. And then the worst-case scenario happened—I saw the sheriff's department boat approach and I saw you. My heart couldn't have beat harder. I was terrified. I knew you were only stopping to assist them. It was easy enough to see their motor had failed. But that could turn deadly and you didn't know what you were up against. I wish I could have warned you, but it was impossible."

"After I stopped to assist them, I saw the weapons. Illegal guns. Machine guns. One of the men tried to reach for one and take us out, but I held him off. And then it all went south." Bree swiped at her eyes. "If only I had listened to Jayce. He wanted to turn around sooner. Get home earlier. Stevie had a birthday party yesterday. I wonder…could Dad have gone ahead without me?" She thrust her head forward and sobbed. "Oh, what have I done? If only we had turned around sooner. I could have been at his party. Stevie and Dad wouldn't be worried. Jayce, Cindy and Taylor would have been there. He would be okay. Maybe those men would never have found you, but now because you helped me, they're onto you."

"I doubt your father had the party without you, Bree. He would have been way too worried. I'm sure the party was postponed. Little Stevie would understand." Maybe not, but her father would have figured out how to appease the child, even in the face of his worst nightmare—possibly losing his daughter, after he'd already lost his son.

Okay. Quinn was done holding back. He took her in his arms, and she willingly leaned into him and sobbed on his shoulder. He settled her against him, allowing her anguish to wash over him, too.

If only he could remove it completely from her.

They both had regrets. She regretted not turning back. He regretted coming here to hide in the first place. But he wouldn't bring that up now and berate himself. She had a lot to work through, including processing how she felt about the man she'd killed back there to save Quinn's hide. Bree could get counseling for that and with help, she'd work through it.

Before she could do any of that, he'd have to get her home and safely back to a family that loved her. What was left of her family anyway, after Steve had died.

And Quinn had left her to deal with her brother's death alone. He'd doomed himself to always be alone. And because of that, he would allow himself to savor this moment with this particular woman in his arms. She was shattered now, but with time, she would recover. After all, she did have a loving family to return to. Little Stevie needed her, and Bree wouldn't let him down.

Quinn would do everything in his power to get her back to Stevie.

"Shh," he whispered. He tightened his hold on her and wished he never had to let go. "You were just doing your job, Bree. You couldn't have known."

She sniffled against him, then freed herself from his embrace. Swiped at her eyes. "Sorry for losing myself like that. Some deputy I am."

"It's okay. You're exhausted. You're allowed to let it out. Besides, it's only me. You know me, and I promise to keep your secret, Deputy Carrington."

"What secret? That I cried on your shoulder?"

He looked at her long and hard and maybe even stopped breathing, then finally, he inhaled and said, "That you're not as tough as you'd like everyone to think. That on the inside, you're a softie as well as a wonderful, loving, caring woman."

She drew in a small breath. His heart ached at the thought of leaving her again.

She peered at him, her beautiful eyes red-rimmed. The way she looked at him—as if she didn't truly know him—pricked a little. He shouldn't expect anything more, but for some insane reason, he did.

"The men with the guns," she said. "I had assumed they were gunrunners. But that wasn't it at all. They had brought the weapons for their own personal use in their search for you. They're hit men."

Ah. Now she was changing the subject. Best for the both of them not to get too personal. He could go along with that.

He nodded. "See what I mean? Brutal." He pushed from the rock and held his hand out to assist her. "Which reminds me why we need to keep pushing to get you back to safety."

"And you, Quinn. We can get you back."

"I already explained to you why I can't go back. I need to remain in hiding. No one can know I'm here."

"But I already do."

He frowned. That could be her death sentence.

SIX

The distant whir of helicopter rotors grew louder, this time drawing closer. Bree whipped her head around to search the sky. There! She saw the bird. This was it. This was their chance! No way would she sit here and do nothing.

She bolted up on the rock, favoring her good leg, and waved her arms. "Hey! Here we are! Please help us!"

"Bree, no!"

"What? I have to let them know I'm here. You can hide in the bushes if you don't want to be seen."

"I already explained to you why this is a bad idea. They aren't the only ones searching. You could draw unwanted attention."

From the woods, bullets sprayed the rock. Quinn yanked her down, igniting a sharper pain in her ankle. She would have fallen off the rock but he caught her and pulled her away from the pile of boulders to find cover in a group of trees.

She gasped for breath. "I didn't think they were that close, but they obviously weren't far behind." Maybe her action was a good thing, after all, because they would have been caught off guard if the thugs sneaked up on them.

"We need to get out of here." He gestured for her to climb on his back.

"Wait. What about your pack? You left it up on the rock."

"It isn't worth a life. Yours or mine. Now let's move it." He almost sounded like a drill sergeant.

After a glance at the sky and the search helicopter that obviously hadn't seen them, she once again climbed onto his back, defeat threatening to overwhelm her soul.

He adjusted her arms around him. "I thought we'd put enough distance between us. We never should have stopped for so long."

"It's my fault. I should have listened. I just… I'm so sorry. I… I want to go home."

To Stevie and Dad.

"I know. And I'll get you there unharmed if you'll follow my instructions."

She felt duly scolded.

If it weren't for Quinn finding her to begin with, she'd be done for. He had to keep up a grueling pace now because of her. Because she'd drawn that unwanted attention he'd spoken of, despite his warning. How utterly disappointing that the searchers hadn't seen her. Noticed gunfire. Had they gotten to Jayce in time to rescue him? If so, then the searchers would be aware of the danger to themselves and also the danger Bree was in every second she remained in this wilderness.

In the meantime, she couldn't do anything except hold on to him, and…well, she could pray. Bree sent up a hundred heartfelt silent prayers for Quinn, for Stevie and Dad, Jayce and his family. And for herself—that she would make it home to her family.

And Lord, maybe You could help Quinn. Help him be able to have a family of his own someday. To love and

cherish a wife and have kids, if that's what he wants.
But I can't stand to see him like this—unwilling to let
himself commit or love.

Quinn's pace began to slow. She knew he was suffering for her. "Let's stop," she said. "Surely we're far
enough ahead that we can rest." Better yet if they lost
those jerks completely. Why had they continued to follow
so long and hard? It seemed crazy that they could even
track them in the dark, especially after Quinn scaled
the ridge.

"We're only a couple of miles out from the edge of
town," he rasped. "I can make it."

He continued over rocks and roots, thick groups of
massive ferns and soft pine needles. Stepped into a small
brook as he crossed, and kept going. Through the trees,
she could see the woods thinned out into a meadow and
on the other side of that meadow, a road. He let her slide
off his back and steadied her.

"I would drop you off at your house if I could. But
it's too dangerous for you to be seen with me."

"The men after me have already seen me with you.
What you mean is *you* don't want to be seen."

He blew out a heavy breath and tugged a cell phone
from his pocket.

She stepped back and onto her throbbing ankle.
What? She couldn't believe it. "You had a cell phone
this whole time? We could have called for help earlier.
We could have let them know where we were so the
helicopter could rescue us."

His blue-gray eyes turned dark and piercing, letting
her know just how much he didn't like the accusing tone
in her voice. "No. We couldn't. You know there's no
signal back there. Here, closer to town, I get a signal."

She didn't feel like backing down. "I think we could have tried."

There. Like it or not, he knew how she felt about it. She could have been trying while she piggybacked. Something.

"We couldn't wait around to be rescued while we were being hunted. Besides, there's no sense in putting anyone else in the line of fire when I could get you safely back. And here you are." He handed the cell over to her. "Call someone to come and get you. I'll wait and watch to make sure you're picked up unharmed."

She squeezed the phone in her sweaty palm, but didn't make the call. Putting a little weight on her ankle, she tried it. It was getting better. Not as bad of a sprain as she thought. So she moved in closer to Quinn.

He grabbed her. "Be careful."

Was that him just wanting her to be cautious on her ankle, or a warning to keep her distance from him?

"No, it's okay. It's getting better. Maybe I could have—"

"Don't be ridiculous. You couldn't have trekked through the wilderness on that."

She wasn't sure what she was doing getting this close to him. Interesting that he didn't step away. Her heart beat an entirely new rhythm as she drew even closer. It was probably a bad idea, but she couldn't help herself. She might never see him again. She might never know if he survived facing off with the hit men after him or found a way to fix what was wrong with his life. And with the knowledge that his life was in danger, Bree could hardly breathe.

She had to try. "Please, Quinn. Don't do this. Let me put you in protective custody." And wouldn't it be nice if she was the one to watch over him? *No. Don't even go there. And no, it wouldn't be nice.* Great. She was arguing with herself.

He grinned. How she'd always loved that grin. "Nice try, Bree. You know why I can't."

"Not really. I know what you've told me, but I think it's just your excuse to stay in hiding. To keep people at a distance. To keep *me* at a distance." Had she really just said that? Bold of her.

He leaned in closer. Close enough to kiss her. Once again, her lungs stilled, but she didn't need oxygen.

She needed Quinn. Did he understand just how much? She didn't understand it herself, because she would never let herself love him—he would only leave. He was leaving now.

"Quinn…"

"I won't put you in danger, more than I already have." His voice was husky.

Her heart tumbled. "I don't want you to disappear again."

He gripped her hands and pressed them against his chest, his heart. "If there were any other way, then I wouldn't have hidden in the first place. I've already told you that someone within the DEA is dirty and news that I'm here could get back to the wrong person. That would definitely put me in danger, but could be even more dangerous for you. Some seriously bad people might suspect you know something about me."

"What could I possibly know?" What wasn't he telling her? "Who is it?"

"I have my suspicions, but I can't prove anything yet. Promise me that you won't give me up. Promise me you'll tell the sheriff you were alone in making your way back."

"I don't know, Quinn. I'm a deputy. That would be

wrong. I would be hiding the truth about what happened out there."

"No, you'd only be hiding the fact that I helped you escape." He released her and stepped back. "If not for me, then do it for Stevie. Don't put him in danger. If the men after me find out about my connection to you, that I…"

"That you what?"

"That I care about you, then they could target you because of that."

Her pulse ratcheted up. He cared about her? She let that idea slide away for now. But more to the point, if what Quinn said was true, then telling the truth could put Stevie and Dad in danger. Still… "What about the fact that those guys are already trying to kill me because of what happened on the river?"

"Low-level people in the organization know they ran into a couple of deputies, that's all. They chased you to cover their tracks. Some of them know that a man helped you. Right now, I'm not sure they even know it was me—the man they were originally coming for. But as for you, they won't mess with you now, Bree. I assure you, they'll let that go. Once you're back in town, they will have lost their opportunity to hide what happened on the river. But if they find out it was me who helped you and learn about your connection to me, then all bets are off. I don't want to risk that. Or confirm to them that I'm even here."

Uncertainty hovered in his gaze. She had a feeling there was something more to this story. Something he was hiding.

"All right. For Stevie." Without question, Dad's and Stevie's lives were worth it. And Quinn's, too. If her keeping his presence a secret would save his life, then she had no choice. But the truth and the fact she'd kept this information from her boss, the sheriff, would come out eventually and she could kiss her promotion good-bye, if not her job.

With a slight limp, she turned away from him. Punched in the number and got Dispatch, and recognized the voice on the other end. Relief swelled inside. "Mel, it's me, Deputy Carrington."

"Bree! Are you okay? Where are you?"

"I'm on the edge of town, but I hurt my ankle and I'm going to need a ride." She gave Mel her location, then ended the call.

She handed the cell back.

That grin again. "Keep it, Bree. You can tell them you couldn't get a signal before now, which is true."

She searched the ground, looked at the road in the distance where she'd soon see help arriving, anything but Quinn's handsome, scruffy face. She felt his eyes on her, so she lifted her gaze to meet his. And asked the question burning inside. A question that she had no business asking because, really, she already knew the answer. "Will I see you again?"

Sirens rang out in the distance. "They're for you," he said.

Without answering, he backed away from her until he was hidden in the trees.

A deputy's vehicle drove down the road and then turned in to the grassy meadow, going as far as it could toward her. She marched forward, with the limp, as best she could. She'd wanted to help him. To protect him. Deep inside she knew that Quinn could protect himself better than anyone else.

He edged deeper into the woods so he wouldn't be spotted and could flee if necessary. He hated doing this to her. Leaving her again. Hated making her keep him out of her report, but he saw no other way.

From a distance, Quinn watched more than one sheriff's department vehicle fly down the road and slow along the meadow, Sheriff Garrison himself included. An ambulance slowed and parked on the shoulder.

He smiled to himself, pushing past the pain of knowing he wouldn't see her again. Bree was getting a big welcome back. They might have even assumed her dead, but now they had beautiful bright-eyed Bree Carrington back. She'd made it out alive and would be hailed a hero.

As she spoke to the lawmen around her, Quinn hoped she wouldn't give him away. He was putting an awful lot of faith in her. He hadn't been completely honest with her. Hadn't told her the full scope of the danger to him. He'd just said enough to ensure she didn't put her own family at risk.

Please, don't tell them, Bree. Remember why it's important to keep my presence to yourself.

Any minute now, he half expected to see her point in his direction and then several heads would turn to look. Would he run and hide like a criminal? He wasn't, but the deputies wouldn't know that until it was much too late for him.

Quinn wasn't exactly sure what he would do if they started marching in his direction. He hadn't expected to be in this position with Bree. When it appeared she'd kept his presence a secret, he relaxed and leaned against a tree, while at the same time remaining aware of his surroundings.

The brutal men after him couldn't afford to come this close to town and the law. That could put their entire mission at jeopardy. That meant it was relatively safe for him to stay here, as long as he remained out of sight of the authorities.

Bree's hair fell over her shoulder as an EMT finished wrapping her ankle, and by the interaction, it appeared she refused a ride to the hospital. She gently eased from the back of the ambulance and instead she climbed into the sheriff's vehicle. Quinn chuckled. The sheriff would have to wipe the mud out, but the man was probably too glad to see his deputy safe and alive to care about the mud just yet.

Well, that was that. Time to turn his attention back to his immediate problem. He made his way deeper into the woods and back the direction from which they'd come. Maybe he could retrieve his backpack. Maybe not. Just because he'd left Bree with the law didn't mean the men had stopped hunting *him.* Eventually they might even figure out he was the one who had assisted the deputy to safety.

He would have to leave Coldwater Bay and find a different place to hide while he figured out how to end this. But he found it hard to focus on his future plans with images of Bree's warm green eyes spinning in his mind. Her red hair, though mud-caked for the most part, spilling over her shoulder. How she felt in his arms when he'd comforted her.

It would take a long time to sweep those images from his mind and heart.

She had asked if she would ever see him again. He hadn't given her an answer because he didn't have one. He'd always left before, but he just didn't want to think of this as the last time he'd see her. Still, when he was with her, she only reminded him of all he could have had but wasn't capable of having.

Would that ever change? Could *he* change? He didn't think so.

Maybe she wouldn't see him, but he would see her. He couldn't leave until he'd made sure she was truly all right, and that nobody was going to come after her to get to him.

That was his greatest fear.

He brandished his weapon as he continued his hike through the woods, every sense attuned to his surroundings. He wouldn't be surprised if he ran into someone who wanted to kill him. Or rather, torture him for information. Maybe take him back. Maybe that was the only way out of this. To face off with Michael Jones—tell him that he was after the wrong person. That Michael had been played.

Another undercover agent had ratted Quinn out because Quinn was too close to discovering what the dirty agent was really up to.

As he hiked, he reached in his pocket for the picture of Bree that he always carried with him. It wasn't there.

His heart skidded. Wait. Had he put that in his pack? *Oh no. No, no, no, no.*

Would the men have cared about going through his gear pack if they came upon it? With as much stealth as he could muster, he made his way back to the place where he'd sat with Bree on the boulder, much too cozy for comfort.

The pack was gone.

He gritted his teeth.

They would find the picture of her. They would know she was important to him.

SEVEN

On the ride to Bree's house, the sheriff told her that Jayce was going to be okay and he'd been the one to let them know where to search for her. The sheriff explained that he had just come back to town to coordinate and bump up their search efforts when he got the call that she was back and okay. The search team had been called off. Another kind of team was preparing to go back in.

Bree immediately thought of Quinn, but her attention shifted to her home as the sheriff steered into the driveway. Bree stepped from Sheriff Garrison's vehicle—stumbled, more like—and caught Stevie up in her arms. He'd run out of the house. Dad lingered near the front door as though he was afraid to believe his eyes.

"I can't carry you, sweetie."

Steve's little boy, her nephew and ward, stared up at her with his big brown eyes. Then he took her all in, including her wrapped ankle. "You got hurt, didn't you?"

"I sprained my ankle."

"Is that why you couldn't make it to the party and we had to wait?"

Bree smiled and ran her hand through his tangled brown hair. She glanced up at Dad, who'd made it out onto the lawn and shaken the sheriff's hand. Bree wasn't sure what Dad had told Stevie so he wouldn't be scared.

Her dad stepped over to them and lifted the boy in his arms. "See, I told you she'd come back. She had something important happen at work."

"And she hurt her ankle," Stevie said. "I don't like your job, Aunt Bree, if it makes you hurt your ankle."

She forced a smile and ignored the look she was getting from her father, who didn't like her job, either. Now she wouldn't hear the end of it. But not yet.

Instead he pulled her into a fatherly hug and whispered in her ear, "I'm so glad you're back." She could swear she heard tears in his voice to join her own.

"Me, too, Dad. Me, too."

He released her. "Let's get you inside to rest that ankle."

Sheriff Garrison squeezed her shoulder. "You take as much time as you need. We'll talk more about everything as soon as you're ready."

She nodded. She'd already told him a version of what had happened. The version without Quinn. The idea that she'd done all of that on her own made her sound like some sort of wilderness survival guide. A hero. And she certainly didn't feel like one, but she wouldn't let that overshadow this moment.

Inside her home, she showered and cleaned up, grateful for the painkillers that made her forget about her ankle. After a long nap, she opened her eyes to see Stevie sitting on the floor watching her.

"Hey, sweetie." She yawned. Was this a dream? Was she still in the woods being hunted?

Was Quinn still with her?

Stevie crawled up onto the bed with her. "Me and

Grandpa made you brownies. He said we have to save the cake. It's in the freezer."

She laughed. It felt good to be home and free and safe and with her loved ones. All she had to do now was keep it that way. Keep them safe. She ruffled his hair. "Okay. I know what you want."

"You do?"

"Yeah. You want to talk about rescheduling the party."

He frowned, a completely unbecoming look for any five-year-old boy. "Not if you don't want to. Grandpa said you need to rest. He said I shouldn't bug you."

She sat up and hugged him to her. "You can bug me anytime you want to. Now, let's go make party plans."

Stevie jumped from her embrace and off the bed. Throwing his arms up, he shouted, "Yippee!"

If only she could have that much energy and be so full of life. If only the light in her hadn't been encroached upon by darkness.

A chill raced up her arms and fear curled around her heart that Stevie could somehow be touched by her nightmare.

Dark circles under his eyes, Jayce produced a weak smile when he saw Bree. He shifted slightly in the hospital bed. Unshed tears burned Bree's eyes. His wife, Cindy, stood next to him, holding his hand. In the other hand she held on to a bouncing baby Taylor, who kept reaching for her daddy.

"Bree, it's good to see you," Cindy said.

Bree approached the bed, careful of her ankle. She took Jayce's other hand. They were more than coworkers. Their families had bonded. Jayce, Cindy and Taylor were like extended family to her, Dad and Stevie.

"I'm so glad you made it out of there." Bree had feared the worst. She glanced at Cindy. How freely could she speak of what happened?

Cindy lifted her chin, seeming to understand. "I need to feed Taylor and change her diaper." She leaned forward and kissed Jayce's forehead—cherishing her husband—and then pressed her lips to his, lingering. Hesitant to leave, she slowly edged away, then walked around the bed to embrace Bree, but Taylor reached for Bree, so she took the baby and held her close.

Her heart leaped; her longing to have a baby one day wouldn't die on its own so easily, even though she had little Stevie.

After a brief cuddle, she released Taylor back into Cindy's arms. Cindy gave Bree the hug she'd intended. Tears shimmered in her eyes. Neither spoke. There were no words to express the fear and terror that had gripped them both at the thought of losing Jayce. No words to express the joy that he'd survived. That they both had survived.

Releasing Bree from the hug, Cindy held Taylor and exited the room, closing the door behind her.

Bree's attention slid to Jayce.

His expression shifted, his features turning somber. "Why'd you do it?"

His anger surprised her. "What…"

"Why'd you draw their attention away like that?"

"You know why. I had to give you a fighting chance. You were injured."

"Bree," his voice croaked. "You risked your life for me."

Gratitude filled his tone and his eyes.

"Of course, Jayce." It had been her only choice. "I couldn't let the men see you were alive. They thought you were dead. I heard them. If they had seen you crawl onto the riverbank, they would have gunned you down. I could see that you were in no condition to run away."

"And you were?" He shook his head. She thought he might cry, too, but he maintained his composure.

"Yes." Even though she'd been shot, too, the Kevlar protected her. She received nothing more than a bruise. That pain had been eclipsed by her sprained ankle. "And I did what had to be done. I'm just glad that you're all right. I saw you were bleeding."

"The first bullet caught me in the chest. Felt like a hammer hitting me. I caught another bullet while in the water. It got me in a vulnerable place—a seam in the Kevlar. I managed to staunch the bleeding. Hide until the search team found me."

"But it was a long wait?"

"I can't really say. It seemed to take forever, but I wasn't really thinking straight. Honestly, I didn't think I would make it. My radio worked so I was able to call for help. But it seemed to take an eternity. I told them about you. That you had drawn the men away."

"How did you know?"

He chuckled. "I knew you'd seen me. I watched you purposefully get their attention. I was so angry at first. You could have stayed hidden, Bree. You risked your life for me." He pursed his lips, then, "Thank you." The words were barely a whisper.

"You're welcome. You would have done the same for me." Despite the painkillers, her ankle throbbed. She eased over to the chair and sat.

"When the searchers didn't find you, I thought the worst. But here you are, Bree. You made it out alive. All by yourself. You are one strong deputy. You deserve that promotion to sergeant. I've already told the sheriff what a hero you are."

A lump swelled in her throat. She wasn't a hero. She'd kept something to herself. Quinn had been there to help her when she fell and sprained her ankle. Even if she hadn't injured herself, she doubted she could have lasted so long without his help. She doubted she would have had the strength to fight off five killers coming after her. She couldn't have seen them in the night without the thermal imaging to track their movements.

No. She was no hero. Without Quinn she would have died. She wanted to share this with Jayce, but what if sharing that information with him put his, Cindy's and Taylor's lives in danger? It seemed counterintuitive to keep the secret, but lives were at stake, so she'd keep his involvement all to herself, though shame threatened to engulf her.

She thought of Quinn slinking back into the woods to hide. Was he all right out there?

Chances were he was long gone.

"Bree? You okay?"

She pulled her gaze from the window where it had drifted with her runaway thoughts. "Yeah, I was just remembering the night."

"Well, maybe we can put all that behind us now. They want to keep me one more night and then I should go home tomorrow. Maybe we should give little Stevie the party he deserves."

"Yes. Definitely. We're already talking about re-scheduling for Saturday if you feel up to it. I doubt the sheriff is going to make you work yet. He insists I take the week off." But that wasn't going to happen.

She remembered back to that moment when she'd

held Stevie in her arms. Dad had hugged them both. He'd actually cried, his head pressed against her hair.

Oh, Dad...

He had always been proud of her but he hadn't wanted her to be a deputy. She'd be putting her life in danger. He'd already lost his son.

She'd disagreed with that characterization of her work, believing she would be helping people. After all, it wasn't like life-threatening situations arose every day, month, or even year. But maybe he was right. Maybe she should find another career. For Dad's sake. For Stevie's sake.

Still... "But you should know, I don't think we can put it behind us just yet. I...shot someone out there. There's a body we need to retrieve, if the men left it behind. And the remaining men could still be in the region. We need to get them if they are."

"Why would they stay behind after what went down?"

The million-dollar question, for which she had an answer that she couldn't tell to anyone. "They had illegal weapons. It could involve drugs. Who knows what else, but they had business here and considering the way they boldly took us out, they aren't too terribly afraid of law enforcement. I'm guessing that if they haven't already, they need to finish their business here before leaving." That harsh brand of criminal element had no respect for the law. No fear.

Jayce frowned. "I can see by that look on your face that you're going back in."

"Yes. I need to show the sheriff where I left the body."

She hoped Quinn was long gone by this afternoon, when a multi-force contingency of law enforcement agencies would comb those woods.

Before last night, she'd never wanted to see him again, but now her traitorous heart wished there were some way to see him. At least some way to know he was safe.

Some way she could warn him to flee.

His growl echoed through the forest. He might as well have drawn a map to show them the best way to hurt him.

Bree could be in mortal danger because of him. If they had the pack, then they would find the picture and know what she meant to him. Keeping her safe was all that mattered now. He'd already gone back to his campsite to see if they'd retrieved their man from the camper.

They had.

They'd trashed the place, too. Sprayed bullets into the camper. Demolished it. He'd have to replace it—and he would, but he couldn't worry about that now.

At least Bree was in town, safe and sound. With her family. A family that would never include him.

Stalking through the forest, watching and listening, he wanted to hit something. Hard.

He was such an idiot! He should never have come back to Coldwater Bay. He should never have kept that picture of Bree. Her beautiful smile. Green eyes. Luscious red hair. The warmth and compassion emanating from her, even in a mere photograph.

It had been a lifeline to him in the darkest of places.

Because of his weakness, his need, now Bree could be in more danger.

Quinn positioned himself behind a group of boulders. In the shade, he wished for a breeze to cool the sweat from his body. Oh yeah, a cold glass of water would be nice, too.

He needed to get sustenance and a source of hydration, but not yet.

He had to protect Bree.

The men hadn't given up hunting him. Add to that if they returned without him, or proof of his death, then their lives were forfeit. They would never give up.

Still, Quinn couldn't flee the area like he had planned and draw them away from Coldwater Bay. That is, not until he could make sure they wouldn't go after *her* to get at him. Getting his pack back before they discovered that picture was key.

The big question: How had they tracked him to Coldwater Bay? He could have been anywhere, but they had found him here, in these woods. They'd come up the river to search—knew he'd been hiding here.

One thing at a time.

He knew what was coming down next. Multiple law enforcement agencies would search the woods for any remaining armed men and the man Bree had killed to save him. He wished he had his binoculars. His thermal imaging. His gear to help him through this.

Now he would find out just how much his skills were worth without the gear to accompany him. He wasn't absolutely positive he could survive this. But he had to. What if Bree needed his protection and Quinn wasn't around to give it?

He needed to get some more gear in addition to getting his own back.

That meant he needed to find one of those men after him and relieve him of his supplies, weapons and ammunitions. Then Quinn could be better prepared to get his stuff and retrieve Bree's picture.

He pushed away from the boulder. Focused his thoughts. He would track those hunting him.

And prepare for the showdown to come, if they collided with law enforcement.

Quinn wasn't entirely sure he could remain undetected if law enforcement combed these woods, but he didn't want anyone else to die because he'd chosen to hide here. He didn't want Bree to get hurt because of him.

In the distance, he heard the familiar drone of a helicopter. He could be grateful that the sheriff's department had not incorporated actual drones in their search. Drones could cover more ground and he might be doomed in his efforts to remain hidden if they were on the hunt.

Quinn stilled. Blended into the forest.

One of Michael's men leaned against a tree and wiped sweat from his brow. Normally, since the men were coming from Louisiana, this Washington weather would be a relief, but not this summer. At least Quinn had military and specialized training, unlike some of Michael's men. He could deal with the weather. He could deal with anything to achieve his objective.

Silently, he crept up behind the man and grabbed him by the throat. Restricted the oxygen to his brain. The man could have fought him a thousand ways, but instinct drove him to fight for his life—to try to relieve Quinn's hold on him with sheer strength. His attempts to free himself failed. Soon his body went limp and Quinn eased him to the ground.

He found something to tie the man in case he regained consciousness before Quinn stripped him of his gear and pack. Soon, law enforcement could capture him. The man would never say a word about Quinn. That would also be a death sentence for *him*.

He searched the man's gear. Quinn's pack wasn't there, nor the contents.

So he'd have to keep tracking them. The sooner he got it, the sooner he could begin leading these guys away from here.

He left the downed man and made his way through the woods to a position that would allow him to see more. He peered through the binoculars that he retrieved from the guy's pack. He spotted boats bringing law enforcement up the river.

And bright red hair shining beneath a sheriff's department cap.

His insides quaked.

Bree. What are you doing?

EIGHT

Tugging her cap down, Bree stepped from the boat onto the pebbled riverbank, minding her ankle. It hurt much less and the swelling was down, but she couldn't let on that it bothered her at all or the sheriff would make her wait in the boat. He hadn't wanted her to come in the first place. But she'd insisted she was their best chance of finding the man she'd killed.

It wasn't like she could look at a map and point out the path she'd taken. She truly wasn't sure where she'd hiked. It had all been a nightmare of running and hiding in the dark. Making her way through a forest maze. Maybe they could have found the body without her help. But she was here now.

Maybe they would find Quinn's camper.

Maybe they would even run across Quinn.

How exactly was she supposed to keep his presence here a secret?

Other law enforcement agencies searched the woods as well—forest rangers and state police. So if he'd stayed around, the chances of his being found were high. But he wasn't a criminal, as far as she knew, so if they found him, it wasn't like they were going to arrest him. He just didn't want the wrong people to find out his location.

But from where she stood, they already knew. There had to be more to the situation that he hadn't shared. Quinn was in even more danger than she realized. What haunted her most was the possibility they would find Quinn's body.

Sheriff Garrison hiked inward with a couple of other deputies, and Bree followed when she probably should have led.

She had to shove the idea of finding Quinn's body from her mind. But she couldn't seem to get it out of her head. And the more she thought about it, the more she realized that if he was dead by the hands of the hitmen, they probably wouldn't leave him behind. She had the sick sense they had to return to Louisiana with evidence of the kill. But it was more likely they would take him back alive to be tortured.

She shuddered, then realized too late that the sheriff had stopped to watch her.

Sheriff Garrison studied her. "You sure you're up for this, Bree? You look kind of pale to me."

While she wanted to present herself as a tough and capable deputy, she had to offer up some truth, or he'd know she was flat-out lying. "Sure. I was up all night, remember? Running from those men. I'm tired. But I can sleep tomorrow when this is over. Right now, I'm worried those guys are still out here."

"I'm sure they're long gone. Why would they stay here with law enforcement scouring these woods?"

"I don't know, Sheriff. Why would they shoot me and Jayce? Why would they track me and try to kill me? I don't think we can just assume we know what they're going to do."

He narrowed his gaze. Had she spoken too harshly to her superior? "I'm sorry, I shouldn't—"

He held up a hand to stop her. "No, you're right. I'd rather you speak your mind to warn us of the danger than hold back."

She nodded. "That's the direction I took off." She gestured the way she'd run, and two deputies hiked on.

God, please keep us safe.

When they came to the copse of trees where she'd hidden, the tree with the hole in it that she'd tucked herself inside, memories flooded her. Terror, too. She swallowed the lump in her throat.

This was the place where she'd first seen Quinn. He'd shown up out of the blue to save her.

Guilt suffused her. She should tell Sheriff Garrison about Quinn.

She heard his voice in her head as if he were standing right there.

...for Stevie. Don't put him in danger...

And she absolutely wouldn't risk Stevie's life. Losing Steve had already crushed them all. Quinn knew that, and he'd known just the right tactic to use. Still, she'd seen in Quinn's eyes his concern for Bree and Stevie, and knew that he'd believed what he'd said to her. Keeping his presence here to herself, at least for the moment, was for the best.

All these thoughts swirled in her head as she hiked in search of the man she'd killed. In search of more thugs, if they remained. Fear tried to turn her back. Fear that those same men would take out more law enforcement.

The tangled and rough land proved too much for her ankle, which began to throb again. Bree pushed through—she had to find the body. Finding that man could go a long way in identifying who these characters were. Quinn might know, but he hadn't shared that information with her. Maybe she could somehow figure this out and help him.

A small part of her hoped she would find Quinn in the woods today so he could be protected. But the way these men boldly shot at two deputies on the river—without fear of consequences—basically confirmed Quinn's assessment that no one could protect him better than himself.

"You okay?" the sheriff asked her again.

She wished he would quit worrying about her. "Sure. We just have to hike up through that narrowing. It was the only path left to me. Somewhere in there is where I shot someone." Defending Quinn.

She'd explained all of it to the sheriff during the debriefing, and though normally she would be given desk duty for a couple of days, her presence was required here before an investigation could be launched into the shooting. Into all of what had happened.

The sheriff nodded and waved for the deputies to continue on, her attempt to redirect him successful.

She blew out a breath, wiped the sweat from her brow and forced herself to keep going. Once they found the body, they could go back. She would soak her ankle and worry about her and Quinn's secret tomorrow.

Hours later, they had trekked and searched the area where she was positive she had dropped one of the thugs.

But no body.

"There's blood here. You can see that." She peered up into the canopy where the sun seemed to beat right through the trees. "His friends obviously took him. Didn't want us to find and identify him and link him to them."

Gunfire thundered much too close.

Heart pounding, Bree crouched next to a tree. The other deputies and the sheriff all did the same, though none of them could be entirely sure from which direction the shots had been fired.

She sucked in air too hard and too fast. Last night barreled into her mind. *Not again.* Bree got a hold of her runaway emotions. *Be the deputy you're trained to be.*

Ignoring her sweaty palms as she gripped her Glock, she peered from behind the tree.

Who was shooting? Quinn at one of the criminals? Law enforcement at Quinn? She should have told them about him.

She would do that as soon as she got the chance. "Sheriff!"

A shadow moved between the trees in the distance. Not Quinn.

No—one of the men from last night. They were still here?

That meant Quinn was still here, too.

A deputy exchanged gunfire with the gunman. Machine guns rattled off. That would draw the other law enforcement, for which she was grateful.

She didn't want to see someone else get shot. Or maybe killed this time.

Bree backtracked to make her way around behind the shooters. She paused between trees and waited. Then continued on.

Hurry—I have to hurry.

Sheriff Garrison. The deputies. They were getting hammered with bullets. Where were the other law enforcement entities?

She slunk behind boulders, crawled over pine needles and through ferns until she was almost behind the shooter with the machine gun. He stopped to reload.

Perfect.

Palms sweaty, heart pounding, Bree positioned herself to confront him. Or shoot him. Her job required her to take someone like this out before he killed. The sheriff and the other deputies probably would have already shot and killed him.

What was the matter with her?

Was she cut out for this job or not?

Arms grabbed her from behind—arms belonging to a big man—and she cried out. He dragged her behind rocks. She caught sight of his brutal, angry, scarred face. He lifted the butt of his weapon.

Bree thought of every evasive move she'd ever learned, but his grip was a steel vise.

A body slammed into him, breaking his hold on her.

Quinn!

He incapacitated the man. Then disabled the man with the machine gun, too.

Quinn rushed to her. "Are you okay?"

"Yes, yes. But what are you doing here? I hoped that you'd be long gone by now." Her heart beat erratically at the sight of him. She was glad to see him. Disappointed, too. He shouldn't be here.

"I had to stay behind. But you have to leave. You shouldn't have come. I think they know, Bree. They know who you are to me. Get out of here now before these men get to you. I'll lead them away from here, I promise. Now get back to your sheriff."

Quinn eyed the woods. The trees that could be hiding someone who pointed a weapon at them now. The boulders behind which he'd been hiding himself could now be sheltering someone else. Someone dangerous.

He should go now. He should really go. But what

about Bree? She was a target here. What had she been thinking to come around behind the shooter? Had her sheriff directed her? He didn't think so. Then again, the sheriff and two deputies had endured a barrage of bullets, and Bree was…well, she was trying to be the hero.

He turned around to face her.

"Please, Bree, get out of here. Go back to your sheriff. I'll watch your back." He couldn't just leave her here until he knew she was safe.

Even if that meant revealing his presence.

"Give me a sec." She grabbed her ankle.

It must still be bothering her. Why had Garrison let her come? Acid burned in his gut.

But what got to him most, the thing that could undo him, was the fact that he wouldn't always be there to save her. He wouldn't always have her back. He wasn't sure he could accept that.

But I have to.

He shook off the craziness exploding in his brain to focus on keeping them alive. He peered down at her, still on the ground. He'd give her a few seconds to rest, like she asked, but the sooner she got back to safety, the sooner he could disappear.

The problem was, Quinn didn't want to leave her ever again, for a hundred reasons that had nothing to do with her safety. But he also needed to lead these men away as they continued to hunt him.

He couldn't do both at the same time.

And yet he knew that leading them away would not ensure her safety. They could always come back—or report their findings back to Jones, who could send another team after Bree. His shoulders sagged. He turned and glanced down at her, and this time she got to her feet. He didn't assist her because he wanted to see that she could do this herself, even if her ankle still bothered her.

Otherwise, he'd pick her up in his arms and march her over to the sheriff himself. A bold thought, that.

He lifted his gaze to look into those heart-melting green, green eyes and lingered there much too long. He pulled his gaze away before he got lost in hers.

His heart pounded with indecision.

With what he shouldn't feel for her.

Her breaths still came hard and fast from fighting. From dodging bullets. From the heat. From this situation.

He wanted to take her away from all this. To escape the ugliness. Except he was the one who brought it with him, and he could never escape it. So getting her away from it—as long as he was with her—wouldn't help her at all.

"Bree," he whispered.

The one word—her name—was met with silence.

Anger burned in her eyes, along with disappointment.

Gunfire in the distance shattered that silence.

Good. The jerks were engaging other law enforcement. That meant they were focused away from Bree. They were probably trying to escape. He hoped they were arrested and made to talk and that the truth would come out about the dirty DEA agent, but that was just a fantasy—these guys probably didn't know about him.

That's why Quinn didn't waste his time with them other than to get his pack back.

Bree hung back and stared at him. What was she waiting for?

He gripped her arms. "Please, just do as I asked. You should never have come back."

"I… I had to make sure they found the body."

His heart tripped up. That was her excuse? "They don't need you for that."

"I wanted to be here in case they found you. To protect."

"But Bree, you don't need to protect me from the law. I'm not a criminal."

"They're searching for men in these woods. You have a gun and a pack, they wouldn't know who you are. I would be here to explain. To tell them the whole truth."

They had so much history, baggage and emotion between them that it was hard for Quinn to let her go. She meant so much to him. Everything.

Which meant he had to convince her that she shouldn't waste her time on him.

He gripped her arms and pulled her closer. "Get this through your head. I do not need your protection. If anything, you've risked my life by forcing me to stay to keep you from getting killed." Well—that part was on him. It was all so convoluted now. He hadn't told her about his stupidity in leaving her picture in his pack.

Hurt poured out from her eyes and seeing that look, being the one to put it there, killed a part of him. Stabbed that part of his heart where Bree would always remain. Good. He needed to be done with this, for her sake.

She twisted out of his grip.

"Fine. Have it your way, Agent Strand. Oh, that's right, you're no longer with the DEA. You couldn't stick with them, either." She gasped, as if realizing she'd said the words aloud. "Oh… Oh, Quinn. I'm so sorry."

She reached for him. He stepped back. Calloused himself. He should have already been immune to Bree.

"Remember, Bree. Not a word about me. Stevie's life could be at risk." *And yours, too.*

The only problem was, if they found the picture of her, Bree's life was already in danger.

And that meant that no matter what he told her, he couldn't leave.

NINE

Moonlight streamed through the bedroom window, keeping Bree awake. She usually preferred total darkness when she slept. But not tonight. Too much fear threaded through her thoughts. Too much apprehension coursed through her veins.

Despite her efforts to relax, her mind wouldn't shut down. Despite her utter exhaustion, her heart rate remained high.

The central air kicked on, startling her. Bree sat up in bed. She peered around her room. No one was here. All was quiet. Except with the AC running, she couldn't listen so easily for anyone who might be stalking the house.

Quinn. He'd done this. He had her scared to death that those men from the wilderness would come for her or Stevie.

It's going to be all right. No one is coming. You're safe.

She spoke to herself the same way she would talk to Stevie. Like a child.

If only the law enforcement contingent had been able to get their hands on those men, but the criminals had slipped through their fingers. Even the guys whom

Quinn took out had disappeared. Granted, the wilderness region wasn't the easiest place to search.

In the meantime, she would remain alert. Hope and pray that whoever was behind these men after Quinn would be brought to justice so that Quinn would be free to live his life without hiding. Free to love. She shook off the errant thoughts, knowing they would lead her to the what-ifs again when it came to Quinn.

He wasn't the guy for her. Had never been and never would be.

And he was the reason she was living in fear.

Her gun rested next to her on the side table within easy reach. She grabbed it and tugged it closer. Tucked it under her pillow, with her hand wrapped around the grip.

Would she ever get back to normal? Physically, she knew she would be okay. Bruises and scratches were already healing. And her ankle wasn't bothering her too much. But her psychological state was a whole other matter.

Who was she kidding? Despite her sheer exhaustion, she couldn't sleep for the violent images of the last couple of days. They filled her mind, setting her on edge. How did she get rid of those images?

Especially images of Quinn.

What a strange way for him to come back into her life—except he wasn't really in her life now. He never had been permanently in her life, even though he'd given her that impression on multiple occasions.

Pain swelled in her throat. She forced her emotions back. She absolutely wouldn't long for him like she'd done at least twice before. If only she could get over him completely. If only she could find someone else.

Her door creaked open.

Bree yanked the weapon from her pillow.

"Aunt Bree?" Stevie's small voice wrapped around her heart.

Oh my... She could have shot Stevie. What was wrong with her?

She quickly hid the gun away, composed herself, then sat up. "Come in, sweetie."

Her brother's five-year-old boy crept into the room, cuddling a black teddy bear. He must have turned on the hall light because it shone into her room. His hair was mussed and his big brown eyes sleepy. He rubbed them as he crawled up onto the bed with her.

She hugged him to her, cradled him on her lap. "What's the matter, sweetie?"

"I had a bad dream."

Wrapping her arms around him, she hugged him even tighter. "I did, too."

He freed himself from her embrace enough to look up in her face. "You did? What was yours about?"

Of course she couldn't tell him about her experience. "I'd rather hear about yours first."

"I dreamed a creepy man was looking through my window."

Bree stiffened. The thought sent chills over her.

"Auntie Bree? What's wrong?"

She finger-combed his hair. "Nothing, punkin. I'm just tired. How about you stay in here and snuggle with me? Maybe then we can both get some sleep."

After settling Stevie in her bed, she slid her gun from its hiding place beneath her pillow. No way could she sleep until she'd checked the house.

Stevie had probably had a dream. But she could picture him seeing the man in his window while he was half-asleep and believing he'd dreamed it. If there was even a chance that was the case, she had to check it out. Stevie had no idea of the reasons Bree was on edge. So she couldn't ignore his dream. What if it wasn't a dream at all? "Stay here, sweetie. I'll be right back."

Safe and sound in her bed, Stevie was already asleep. She smiled to herself. Bree would need to check on Dad, too, but didn't want to wake him. Leaving the hall light on, she continued quietly toward the kitchen, limping only a little.

It was only a dream. No one was looking in Stevie's window. She repeated the words to settle her nerves.

Regardless, she had to check.

The door to his room was ajar. His bedsheets crumpled. She crept into his room, avoiding the moonlight, and peeked out the window. No one was out there. And even if they had been, they wouldn't still be in that spot.

Next stop, Dad's room. Bree made her way there. She could hear his snoring through the walls. She quietly opened the door and glimpsed inside.

All seemed perfectly normal and secure. It wasn't like they had left windows open because of the unusual heat.

Now to check the rest of the house. When she was finished, she'd get a glass of warm milk to help her sleep. She wasn't sure it would actually work, but Mom used to tell her it would.

Still, no milk until the house was cleared. And it was only a dream. Everything was fine.

Bree kept her gun at the ready—after what she'd been through, she couldn't possibly discount Stevie's dream no matter what she told herself. She had to be sure her family was safe before she would let her guard down.

She cleared the living room, dining room, kitchen and breakfast nook. At the back of the house, she found a curtain billowing. The window was open. Fear strangled her but there was no time to be paralyzed. She kept her wits about her.

Had Dad left it open? She was sure she had checked and locked them up before going to bed. Had turned on the alarm system, though, as a deputy, she knew there were ways to disarm any alarm if a criminal was so inclined.

Goose bumps crawled over her. She closed and locked the window. Gripping her weapon, she lifted the gun, held it at the ready and whipped around. Was someone in the house?

Bree cleared every room again like she'd been trained and found no one. She breathed a sigh of relief, but still remained on guard.

Forget the milk. She just wanted to snuggle Stevie. Hold him close and keep him safe.

Back in her room, she found Stevie still sleeping soundly. She needed to protect him, so she kept her gun close, but hid it away where she could reach it easily on the other side of her—opposite where Stevie slept.

Then she closed her bedroom door.

A hand pressed over her mouth.

"You care about the boy, so you won't scream," the gravelly voice whispered. "Understand?"

She vehemently nodded as tears surged. She held them back. She wouldn't show weakness.

"Where is it?"

She shook her head. Where was what?

He slowly removed his hand and came around to face her, backing her into the corner. She'd seen his face now. That was never a good thing. She'd seen the faces of the men on the river, too, but this—somehow, she knew seeing this man's face was much different.

He gripped her arms, hurting her. "Where is the money he stole?"

"Who...who stole? What are you talking about?" Fear gripped her. She had no idea what this man wanted and feared if she couldn't produce it, then he would kill her or hurt Stevie.

"Your friend Quinn. He stole money from my boss."

Quinn, a thief? The news stunned her. Not the best time for her to find this out. "He didn't leave it with me. I don't know anything." *Please believe me!* She'd just given away that she knew Quinn, but it would have been pointless to try to deny it.

The man pursed his lips. "I believe you. You wouldn't risk the life of the child."

Stevie's life? The man would take his life? *Quinn, what have you done?*

"But you know where *he* is."

She shook her head and hoped he believed her on that, too. "I don't know anything about him. I don't know where he is."

His eyes narrowed with suspicion. He didn't believe her this time. "Find him. Lead me to him or else I'll hurt someone you love."

"But how—"

"He stole from the man I work for. That's a death sentence. I won't return without Quinn Strand. You have twelve hours to find him."

"You can't expect me to find him. He was in the woods. He disappeared. I can't possibly—"

He slowly walked over to Stevie and stood over him. No...

"How...how do I find you?" Her voice crackled with weakness.

"You don't. I know you're a deputy, so that makes

what I'm about to say next ironic. Don't call the police." He snickered, but then his expression went grim. Deadly. "You won't like the consequences if you do," he reminded her.

Bree believed him. She fought to keep her knees from giving out. What kind of deputy was she? She couldn't even protect her family. He wasn't intimidated by her in the least—threatening a deputy!

Then, just like that, the man was gone. He left her house as silently as he'd come in.

Bree let herself crumple to the floor and sob, her cries fueled by fear for Stevie and anger at Quinn. That's why they wanted him—he'd stolen their money. *How could he do this?*

On her knees, she let her quiet sobs free. A hand touched her shoulder. She jerked back ready to defend herself.

Stevie!

Oh, Stevie… She could have hurt him.

"Why are you crying?" he asked in a sleepy voice. "Did you have a bad dream again?"

She sniffled and nodded. Tugged the boy to her and hugged him like she would never let go, sniffling the tears away. She was so glad he hadn't woken up when that man had stood over him. The man he'd seen in his window and had attributed to a dream. Stevie might never get over that if he truly understood what he'd seen.

How did she make this go away?

Oh, Lord, what am I going to do?

She lifted Stevie as she climbed to her feet, ignoring the slight pain in her ankle, holding him tightly. Her hands trembled, and she hoped he wouldn't notice that as she carried him over to the bed. Pulled back the cover and let him crawl inside. She had only imagined he was safe in this house and in her bed, and that she could adequately protect him.

She'd been a fool.

"Get some sleep." Bree kissed him on the forehead. "Good night, sweetie."

She turned away before he could see more tears. She had no idea what to do now. Desperation flooded her quivering heart and mind.

Think, Bree.

She had to toughen up or they wouldn't survive this.

The men after Quinn knew she was somehow connected to him. But for some reason, they seemed to believe that he had stolen money and given it to her, a deputy, of all people! It was exactly what Quinn had warned her about. It was all happening like he had feared it would. She was paying a high price for her connection to a guy who said he cared about her, but always left when they got too close.

These men had figured out that she was a way for them to get to Quinn. They would use her to get what they wanted, and she would go along with it because they knew she would do anything for Stevie.

She stood in the shadowed corner of the room where the man had sneaked up behind her. How utterly stupid of her to leave Stevie in here alone while she went to check the house. He'd come into this room while she was gone. He could have hurt Stevie.

Fury snuffed out the tears that might have fallen.

And she'd let that happen. She hadn't even thought to clear this room—the corners, the area behind the door.

Because she'd been careless, she was now stuck in a situation where she had to track a man whom even professional killers hadn't been able to locate. And even if she found him, what then? Did she honestly believe that turning him over would secure her family's safety?

Of course not. She wasn't that naive. Even if she knew where to find Quinn, they would kill her if she handed him over to them. Maybe Stevie and Dad, too. She'd seen too much. She knew too much.

She eased into the plush chair and pulled a pillow to her while she watched Stevie sleep, oblivious to the danger around him. To the threats against him. She thought back to the life she'd been living only a few days ago.

The warm summer days. The job that had given her satisfaction. A potential for growth. A future. And then Stevie's birthday party—the one she'd had to reschedule.

"This coming weekend," she'd told him repeatedly.

But that wasn't going to happen now. Bree knew what she was going to have to do.

Quietly, so she wouldn't wake Stevie, she opened the closet and pulled out clothes. She got dressed and headed to the room she and her dad used as an office, flipping all the lights on as she went. No one was going to grab her from the shadows ever again.

Bree sat at the desk in the small office and opened her laptop. The mini blinds were closed so no one could see in the house or watch what she was doing. She started looking for airline tickets. She didn't care how much it cost; she wanted the next flight out for Dad and Stevie. Dad could take Stevie away to see relatives in Idaho. He'd been talking about wanting to see family there for a while. He'd taken early retirement but freelanced as a programmer, working as little or as much as he wanted. Now was his chance to take the trip. She could offer it to him as a surprise pre-birthday gift, since his birthday was next month.

Or…she could tell him the truth.

Maybe both.

But she absolutely couldn't risk Stevie's or Dad's life while this situation was still so tense and dangerous.

And she had every intention of reporting what happened to Sheriff Garrison.

The truth. All of it.

Even the part involving Quinn, because he was the center of this case. Though she'd been warned not to contact the police by the man here tonight and by Quinn, with this turn of events, she'd be a fool not to make the most of every resource she had.

She pressed her fingertips against her eyes, hoping to stop more tears that surged as the man's words about Quinn came back to her. The man had actually thought that she'd hidden the money Quinn had supposedly stolen from his boss.

She'd been hurt and shocked at his words. And hadn't believed them. At first.

But they made sense. Quinn had said that his cover had been blown and he'd gone into hiding to figure out who within law enforcement was behind it all. Maybe the missing money was part of the frame-up…but she had to consider the other possibility, too. Could he have been lying about all of it? Could he have insisted she not reveal his presence because he truly had broken the law?

She didn't know what was true—except that the danger was very real. Quinn didn't seem to believe that anyone in authority could be counted on. Was there a warrant for his arrest? She hadn't thought to look! She hadn't had time. Maybe he was telling the truth about a dirty DEA agent, and maybe this agent was involved, connected to the criminals somehow, and maybe if the

DEA got their hands on Quinn, he could be in danger that way.

But Bree knew that Sheriff Garrison could be trusted. She trusted everyone in her department.

Without a doubt.

Why hadn't she trusted them to begin with? Because she'd wanted to give Quinn the benefit of a doubt, that's why. Now she questioned that decision.

A branch scratched the window.

Fear coursed through her again. She gripped her weapon, desperately wanting to check on Stevie again. Peering out the window, she saw nothing, so she headed back to her bedroom. She glanced at Stevie, still sleeping soundly. She released a sigh of relief.

Still… She crept to her window and peeked out.

Quinn stood in the shadow of a tree.

TEN

Frogs croaked from a nearby pond as he waited in the darkness under the tree. Here in this pleasant neighborhood, he could almost imagine himself living a normal life. Going to work in the morning and coming home in the evening to eat dinner with a family he cherished. He imagined himself holding Bree in his arms without another care on earth.

That was another world. Another Quinn. A Quinn who didn't have to sneak around in the middle of the night so he wouldn't be seen.

He couldn't exactly approach Bree in broad daylight, so the wee hours of the morning would have to do. The curtains moved in the window. She'd seen him. He had hoped he wouldn't have to actually knock on the front door to get her attention. Now for more waiting. Would she come out to meet him?

The front door creaked open. Quinn jogged quietly over and slipped inside the house, into the brightly lit foyer. He squinted in the sudden brightness.

The house smelled of apples and cinnamon. Of home and love and family. His chest constricted.

Fully dressed as though she'd been up, Bree pressed a finger to her lips, then led him through the house to the garage. After she shut the door behind him, she flipped on the fluorescent lights.

Her eyes wide, she pressed her forefinger into his chest. "What are you doing here? Are you crazy?"

"I needed to warn you."

"You couldn't have just called?"

"You're right. I should have." He *was* crazy. "But I wanted to see you to make sure you listened to what I have to say."

"You're too late in warning me." Fear edged her tone.

His heart jackhammered. "What do you mean?"

"Someone was here." She broke down then. She pounded his chest.

Dread filled him. Her punches didn't hurt him physically. No, they were much more painful than that. He took all she gave him. Though he wanted to know what had happened, he let her get her fury out. Then when she was done, he held her in his arms. He'd imagined doing this only moments before, but that had definitely been a different set of circumstances—another world. And now he'd dragged Bree into his.

Bree shoved away from him. Stepped back.

"Bree, what happened?"

"Someone was here, Quinn. Someone broke into the house."

"No…"

"He threatened me. Threatened Stevie. Tell me you didn't do it."

"Didn't do what? Bree, what are you talking about?"

"He wanted to know where it was."

Quinn stiffened. "Where it was?"

"He said you'd stolen from his boss."

What… He stumbled backward.

"Is that true, Quinn? Did you steal from them? Is that why they tracked you all the way to my backyard?"

"No. Absolutely not. How could you even think I'd steal drug money?"

"Well, I don't know. Maybe because you're running from the law, too. You're hiding. You were so insistent that I tell no one that you're here—not even the sheriff. What am I supposed to think?" She pressed her hands against her face as if to cry, but quickly dropped them. "I've been such a fool to listen to you. Now when I tell the sheriff the truth, he'll think I was aiding a criminal. I might even lose my job. Because of you, Quinn."

Wow. He really was the pain-maker. He hadn't realized just how important it was for Bree to believe him. To believe *in* him. How could that be when he'd repeatedly distanced himself from her, knowing that he couldn't be the man she needed? The friend she needed?

He needed someone to believe in him, though.

And the most important someone in his life was Bree.

"I know it's not enough to say I'm sorry that someone broke into your house and threatened you, that I brought any of this on you." He approached her, hands out.

"You stay away from me. You can't be here. You have to go, Quinn. I'll figure something out, but he could already know you're here and come barging into this house. Kill you and all of us." Her voice pitched higher with her panic.

But how did he calm her? Get her to listen to reason?

"No one is out there. I scouted the area. He was just scaring you, threatening you." Though he probably would be watching again later. Quinn had very little time. Why had he come here? He'd only put everyone in more danger. Himself included.

She backed all the way to the wall as he approached. The light flickered above them, startling both of them. Entirely too much fear and tension filled this garage. He drew in a calming breath. He had to convince her. Looking into her eyes, he hoped to find something there he could latch on to. Some connection from their past.

"You know me. I would never do that. I didn't steal someone's money."

In her eyes, he saw that she wanted to believe him, but was wary. "Then why did he say that?"

He shook his head as he considered the reasons. "I honestly don't know. Remember, these are drug dealers. Murderers. You can't believe anything they say. The way I figure it, someone told them I had stolen the money so that increased their need to find me—and put an even higher price on my head."

"So you knew about this. You knew they thought you'd stolen from them."

"No. But it doesn't surprise me." This had to be Declan Miller's doing—the agent he suspected. They were onto him now, so he used Quinn as a scapegoat.

Bree studied him as if she was deciding if she believed him or not. "Is there anything else you haven't told me?"

That I had a picture of you that was my lifeline in Iraq—and that picture could be what led to that break-in tonight. That I could never get you out of my head no matter how far away I traveled around the world. No matter the darkest places I've been. But he wouldn't tell her that. That information was his alone.

"I didn't want you to worry. I wanted to get you back here where you'd be safe and then lead the men away."

"But you haven't led them away."

"No, because now they're onto you. And that means you're not safe, but you already know that."

"Which is why you shouldn't be here." There it was in her eyes. A softening. Emotion. Connection. It all surfaced. She *did* believe him.

Why did he put so much importance on that when her life was in danger? Stevie's and her father's, too.

Suddenly she rushed forward and wrapped her arms around him. Hugged him so hard, he thought he would break. He savored it. It could be the last time he saw her—it *should* be. He needed to leave her alone. If only he hadn't come to Coldwater Bay to begin with. But he'd quit rehashing that. It was too late. Instead, he'd just take this moment to enjoy having her in his arms.

When she loosened her grip, he gently held her close so she couldn't escape and peered into her pretty face. The smattering of freckles across her nose. Her beautiful, compassionate green eyes. He wanted to run his fingers through her mussed red hair. But more than that, he wanted to see that she truly believed him. Believed *in* him. That she trusted him.

Why he would expect that much after what he'd done to her, he didn't know. But it was the one thing he needed.

"I promise you, Bree. I didn't break the law. I'm not a criminal." He calmed his nerves before she heard his shaky voice. "I can never take back what's happened. I regret a lot of it—especially that you're involved now. For that I'm so sorry. More than anything I need you to believe me."

She nodded slightly and lifted her chin. Her mouth was so near his, her breath feathered his face. And her lips drew him in until he was kissing them. Gently at first, then with more emotion than he should ever feel for Bree Carrington. She grabbed his head and edged him closer, showing him how much she cared, too.

With her in his arms, for this moment in time, she was his alone. He drew in the essence of all that was Bree. He'd kissed these lips before. Memories of kissing her flooded through him. She was a tough deputy, but also an utterly amazing woman. Hope for something lasting between them this time sent a pang through his heart. Hope for something he could never have with her. He had to calm himself and pull away from being wrapped up in Bree. He eased back slightly, not willing to let go completely. A quiet tenderness passed between them. He couldn't step away if he wanted to.

I can't do this to her. Lead her on and then leave her again. I won't.

And Bree knew that score. She wasn't likely to play this game with him, which is what left him baffled that they'd ended up like this again, inexplicably wrapped up in a kiss. Desperation and fear had bashed in the barriers he'd put in place.

Neither of them would cross the lines they'd drawn—beyond this kiss. A moment of weakness. That's all this was.

And he couldn't afford any more of them.

She broke off the kiss. Appeared to shake off the hold he'd had on her as she stepped from his embrace.

"Quinn... You need to leave." She appeared to contemplate her next words. "Stevie's life is in danger if I don't turn you over to them. If they find out you were here, I don't know what they'd do. You should go now, Quinn. And never come back. Because if I don't know where you are, then I can't tell them."

* * *

Emotions—the good kind and the bad kind—fought for control in Bree's chest. She slowed her breathing. Gained her composure.

What *had* she been thinking? Maybe the desperation in his eyes, the need for her to believe him, had hooked some part of her heart that still clung to him. But that was all her heart. As for using her head, well, she hadn't. But that's how she was when she was near Quinn. A woman without a brain.

The way he kissed her just now—like he'd never kissed her in the past—let her know that it had moved him, maybe as much as it moved her. She couldn't so easily shake how he made her feel.

Even though they could never be a couple. He would never be the man for her.

She took another step back to put more distance between them and clear her head. The pain in his eyes was almost unbearable. "You're a good man, Quinn. I'm sorry I ever doubted that for even a minute, but I have to think of Stevie and Dad."

"Don't forget yourself, Bree. You have to think about protecting yourself, too." He jammed his hands in his pockets and slunk toward the door as if to leave.

Good.

Not good.

"If they see you here, Quinn, then we're all in trouble."

"To be safe, you need to leave Coldwater Bay. At least for the short term."

"I'm already making plans. I was on the computer buying tickets for Dad and Stevie to go visit family."

"But you're staying."

Get Up To 4 Free Books!

Dear Reader,

IT'S A FACT: if you answer 4 quick questions, we'll send you 4 FREE REWARDS from each series you try!

Try **Love Inspired® Romance Larger-Print** books featuring Christian characters facing modern-day challenges.

Try **Love Inspired® Suspense Larger-Print** novels featuring Christian characters facing challenges to their faith... and lives

Or **TRY BOTH!**

I'm not kidding you. As a leading publisher of women's fiction, we value your opinions... and your time. That's why we are prepared to reward you handsomely for completing our mini-survey. In fact, we have 4 Free Rewards for you, including 2 free books and 2 free gifts from each series you try!

Thank you for participating in our survey,

Pam Powers

To get your 4 FREE REWARDS:
Complete the survey below and return the insert today to receive up to 4 FREE BOOKS and FREE GIFTS guaranteed!

"4 for 4" MINI-SURVEY

1 Is reading one of your favorite hobbies?

☐ YES   ☐ NO

2 Do you prefer to read instead of watch TV?

☐ YES   ☐ NO

3 Do you read newspapers and magazines?

☐ YES   ☐ NO

4 Do you enjoy trying new book series with FREE BOOKS?

☐ YES   ☐ NO

Please send me my Free Rewards, consisting of **2 Free Books from each series I select** and **Free Mystery Gifts**. I understand that I am under no obligation to buy anything, as explained on the back of this card.

☐ **Love Inspired® Romance Larger-Print** (122/322 IDL GNPV)
☐ **Love Inspired® Suspense Larger-Print** (107/307 IDL GNPV)
☐ **Try Both** (122/322/107/307 IDL GNP7)

FIRST NAME	LAST NAME

ADDRESS

APT.#	CITY

STATE/PROV.	ZIP/POSTAL CODE

She nodded. "Yes, and you should know I'm going to tell Sheriff Garrison the truth about what happened."

"I see."

"I have no choice. That man who broke in tonight also warned me against telling the police. But that just reminded me that I *am* the police. I'm going to do my job and catch these guys."

Quinn had half a foot out the door. Did he think she was going to detain him? Sure. *Go ahead and leave when things get tough. You always do.*

"Just go, Quinn. I need to get my family somewhere safe."

"I'm not going too far, Bree. We need to stay in touch. I'll let you know what I find out about who is behind this."

"You do that. Good idea. Just be sure not to tell me where you are. I'll tell my boss that I'm working with you to find out who is behind this. Not that that will help my case any."

He hung his head, lingering. "He'll understand you hesitated because you were afraid for your family, Bree. He's a family man, too."

He approached her again and lifted her hand. Turned it over and pressed a cell phone in her palm. "You can contact me with this. Give me up if you must. I'll give myself up—but I need to look into a few things first. I'm formulating a plan."

Bree eyed the cell, then held it out to him. "I don't want this. If I have it then I have no excuse to give them that I don't know how to find you. They could force me to call you and set up an ambush. Something. No. I won't take this."

"You don't have a choice. I want to know what happens next. I want to know if you need me."

If she needed him? She gasped for breath. She needed him like a hiker needed a snakebite. Her traitorous heart had a different idea about her need for Quinn, but she wasn't listening tonight.

He started to go out the door, but hesitated. Then stuck his head back in. "You're doing the right thing."

Then he disappeared.

She realized she still held the cell phone. "Wait… Quinn…"

But he was gone, and she wouldn't chase him down to give him the phone.

Lord, please help me through this.

New images of Quinn now crept in and superimposed over the old one of him holding her brother—gone to this world.

She rubbed her arms to chase away the goose bumps that seemed to come and go far too often of late.

Time to get busy. Get her family up and out of here.

Back inside the house, she headed down the hallway to Dad's room first to wake him, though it was much too early. But this was urgent. How did she explain this?

She made to knock on his door, then smelled coffee just as she sensed a presence behind her.

"Bree," her father whispered behind her.

She released a sigh, then turned to face him. "Dad. You scared me."

Though he held a cup of coffee, she rushed to him and threw her arms around him.

He hugged her back. "Bree, what's this all about?"

Not ready to get Stevie up yet, she stepped back and led Dad to the kitchen. Bree pressed her face to her hands. Where did she even start?

"Just take a deep breath, honey, and tell me what's got you so frazzled."

Bree dropped her hands. "Why are you up so early?"

"I could ask you the same thing, but the truth is I heard you in the house. I couldn't sleep so I got up early and made myself a cup of coffee. I see it was the right decision. Now, please tell me."

"You know how you've been wanting to go to Idaho to visit your aunt Gina?"

He lowered his cup. "Yeah?"

"I just bought you and Stevie tickets. Your flight leaves in five hours."

"What? Bree, why would you do that? Sure, I've thought about going, but not right now. You just got back. Stevie's birthday party is soon. No one there knows we're coming and I'm not ready to go. I haven't packed my bags. What's going on?"

"Your lives are in danger, Daddy. A man was in the house this morning. He threatened me."

"And you're sending us away but you're not coming?"

"I'm staying here."

"I absolutely won't leave you here to go through this alone. Either you come or I stay."

"What do you think you can do, Dad? I'm law enforcement. I'll have all the backup I need. But Stevie... He's just a child. The man threatened Stevie. So you're going to get on that flight and protect your grandson."

Grim lines carved through his face as understanding took hold. He had no choice. Stevie was depending on them to keep him safe. Dad slowly nodded. She thought she saw tears forming in his eyes.

Oh, Daddy...

Bree wished she could go with him. That they could all just leave the danger behind.

"You should know, too, that I was warned against telling the police of the threats."

"But you're going to anyway."

"Yes. I have no choice."

"What do they want from you?"

Her father didn't know yet that she'd run into Quinn while escaping the wilderness. Quinn had saved her out there. Dad wouldn't have wanted to hear that. He had never liked Quinn because he'd broken Bree's heart, and he probably held him somewhat responsible for Steve's death. Dad wasn't going to like the answer she gave him.

"Quinn Strand, Dad. They want Quinn Strand."

ELEVEN

At the county sheriff's department, Bree forced herself down the hallway toward Sheriff Garrison's office. Deputy Bobby Woodbridge stopped her before she reached the door. He'd always liked her. "Hey, Bree. What are you doing back? Sheriff gave you a week off."

She knew he cared about her as a person and hoped for more between them, an affection she didn't particularly return. She didn't stop as she passed him, saying, "I'm here to talk to him."

She forgot about Bobby and focused on her mission. *I can do this. I have to do this.*

At his office, she lingered in the doorway, knowing the sheriff wouldn't want to see her, but hoping for an invitation to come inside.

Sheriff Garrison was on the phone. He eyed her. Scrunched his face as if to ask, "Why are you here?"

She'd have to wait until he finished the call, so she stepped back and leaned against the wall, letting his unspoken question swirl around in her head. That's exactly what she was asking herself, only with a completely different perspective. She'd botched everything, starting with the encounter with criminals on the river that had almost gotten both her and Jayce killed. She should have been more cautious. Should always keep her guard up, but she had been unprepared, at best. That wasn't even counting the fact that she kept to herself that Quinn had been involved.

Her gut soured. She hadn't been able to eat a thing, though she'd tried. She'd needed the energy to power through the strain of the day, but her mind and body wouldn't cooperate.

The next hour or so might change her life completely. She pushed past the nausea in her stomach and the tightening in her throat and faced the reality that she could possibly walk out of here without a job.

"Bree." The sheriff's gentle voice startled her.

She offered a tenuous grin. "Sheriff."

"Come on in." Standing in the hallway next to his office, he gestured wide for her to step inside.

His expression revealed compassion and concern for her, even though he had so much going on with what had happened out there yesterday. They still hadn't caught the men who had attacked her and Jayce. They could still be out there.

"Have a seat."

She wasn't sure she could do this sitting, but eased into the chair anyway.

"I gave you the week off to recuperate. And by the look on your face, you're not even close to recovered. Now what's bothering you?"

Her frown was painfully deep. "There's something I didn't tell you about what happened."

The sheriff eased into his seat behind his desk. Steepled his hands. "I'm listening."

"Those men out there, they were after Quinn Strand."

His eyes were laser focused on hers. "Tell me everything, Bree."

So she did. She laid out the details as they really happened. Unfortunately, though she tried to explain in her most professional deputy voice using law enforcement words, she couldn't stop her eyes from tearing up. At least those tears hadn't streamed down her cheeks. Yet.

"I'm so sorry for keeping this from you. I guess I'm not deputy material after all, Sheriff."

He said nothing at all. Just leaned back in his chair, clasping his hands over his midsection, and studied her.

"I can see how you thought you were doing the right thing—protecting Stevie. Even protecting Quinn. Given the circumstances, I'm not sure I would have reacted any differently. I might have taken the time to think it through before coming to the police if my wife or child or grandchild were threatened. And you've done that, Bree. You've thought it through and even with the additional, personal threat on your life and Stevie's, you've come to me now."

"So...you aren't mad?"

"If I were to be angry at anyone, it would be at Quinn Strand for putting you in this position. But then again, he didn't have to step in and expose himself to save your life." The sheriff sighed. "I'm not sure how the other agencies involved will see it, but that's their problem."

"You're not firing me?"

"Firing you?" He frowned, then angled his head. "I don't have enough smart, able-bodied deputies as it is. Why would I fire one of my best? Let's just be clear going forward—please come to me with what you learn. You can trust me. I would never put your family in danger."

She nodded, taking in all his words. Hoping they would change how she felt about herself right now. This had gone so differently than she had imagined. Still, it wasn't something she could celebrate yet. This wasn't over. Not by a long shot.

"Thank you, Sheriff. I appreciate you believing in me."

"Bree, that's what family does. This county sheriff's department is a kind of family." He toyed with a blue glass paperweight on his desk, then looked up at her. "So you got Stevie and your dad off on a plane. Let's hope and pray that they'll be safe in Idaho."

Bree could hope that some distance would protect them, sure, but these guys came all the way to Washington from Louisiana for Quinn.

"I guess you don't want to take some time off, given the circumstances."

"No. I want to work. I want to find out who these guys are who have threatened me and my family." And help Quinn. He wouldn't share that information because he didn't want her to put herself into more danger.

"I have an assignment for you. When Quinn contacts you again, and I have no doubt that he will, try to talk him into meeting. Just you, me and Quinn. I don't doubt his concerns that someone on the inside could locate him, but I figure they already know he was here by now via their drug running contacts. I want to find out what we can do to help him with the men after him."

"I'll work on that." Bree stood, feeling lighter than she had in days, though a dark cloud of trouble still hung over her. Maybe she could push it completely away and they would resolve this soon. "I'm going to run home for a bit. Just going to grab some coffee and breakfast. I haven't eaten this morning. Couldn't. But now I feel better. Thank you for being so understanding. We'll get to the bottom of this. I'll be back up here within the hour."

"Take your time. I think it would be best if you could

take the week off like I told you, but I understand that you wouldn't be able to get any rest until this is over anyway. And yes, we will get to the bottom of this, Bree. Just remember that you can trust your fellow deputies and your sheriff to have your back. Now, keep up the good work, but... Don't forget to take your time. Set up an appointment with the counselor, too."

"Will do." She left his office and was about to head out the door when she decided to grab coffee in the kitchen for the short drive home, even though the department's coffee wasn't the best. She needed the caffeine. She spotted a box of doughnuts and grabbed a maple-covered one. Not the best breakfast, but maybe she could eat the doughnut as a way of a small celebration. She'd kept her job. She was in the middle of taking a bite when she heard voices in the hallway.

Chewing the doughnut, she hesitated and remained in the kitchen. She'd never been one to eavesdrop, but she wanted confirmation that the deputies and sheriff truly had her back, and that she could trust them in this unusual predicament. It involved her family, after all.

"We're going to get our man," the sheriff said. "Quinn Strand is behind this. I just got a report this morning that there's a warrant out for his arrest for stealing drug money. Bree is going to bring him to us. Be aware, she doesn't know that's what she's going to do. Quinn has some kind of hold over her, and she needs us to free her and arrest Quinn. Once he's in custody, the threats on her life and her family's life will be extinguished."

The morning was getting away from him and all he'd managed to do was hole up in a cheap motel. No need to stay in the woods—that cover had been compromised. Plus, disappearing from that area would mean the men

after him would leave as well, and no more deputies
would be in danger as they continued their searches.
Unfortunately, Jones's men remained in Coldwater Bay
waiting on Bree to turn him over one way or another.

Quinn stared at the cell on the table, considering
all the possible scenarios and outcomes. He hadn't recovered the backpack and her picture, but things had
escalated anyway. The pack, her picture, didn't matter anymore.

They knew.

Michael Jones knew.

Bree was important to Quinn. She'd already been
threatened. And Quinn should have stopped this long
before that.

He thought about the call he needed to make to his
boss, Stan Rollins, at the DEA. He never intended for
things to go this far. For anyone to be caught in the
middle or hurt.

He thought back to that moment he'd been about to
step out of his car to meet up with his "friends"—those
he'd befriended during his time undercover within the
drug trafficking organization. A transfer of a half a million dollars' worth of drugs was going to take place.
His job wasn't to arrest anyone but to report back—
they wanted enough information and evidence to bring
down the whole organization. That kind of operation
took years. Unfortunately, he discovered another agent,
Declan Miller, and suspected he wasn't playing by the
rules. Declan worked directly under Michael Jones, who
was only a leader over the New Orleans region. Quinn
suspected Declan, who had moved up in the ranks, was
taking money and drugs for himself. Unfortunately,
Declan was related to a higher-up in the DEA.

That didn't work out in Quinn's favor.

And maybe…just maybe, that had been the whole reason he'd been assigned to work undercover—someone had suspected Declan had gone to the dark side, but they wouldn't suggest it, considering the man's connections. Just plant another agent within the organization and hope that eventually the truth would come out.

Seconds before Quinn was about to exit his car, he received a text from a DEA informant that Quinn had been made.

His cover had been blown.

He'd sat in his vehicle, weighing his options. Who knew? Everyone? It seemed clear that Declan had ratted him out, but Quinn hadn't been able to get evidence about everything Declan had done before he went on the run. Declan couldn't continue working both sides of the law with another undercover agent in his backyard, so to speak. So get rid of Quinn and Declan was safe.

In his gut, Quinn had known that if he walked in, he wouldn't walk out alive.

The muzzle of a gun had pressed against the window of his car door, aiming at his head, at the same moment he'd shifted into Reverse. He peeled out and away from the parking lot, escaping.

Images of that day accosted him. He'd barely escaped with his life. Quinn bolted to his feet and paced to shake the memories off. That was then. This was now. And enough was enough.

He couldn't let Bree suffer any more because of him. He couldn't resolve this any other way. He had to come forward with his suspicions, though he had no evidence to back them up, and he would take the risk that he would be believed over Declan.

Or he would lose his life.

He reached for the cell to make a call, but it rang with an incoming call.

Quinn answered the cell phone, surprised to hear from Bree already. His heart rate kicked up. What had happened now?

"Quinn, is that you?"

"Yes."

"I have some bad news."

His gut clenched. "Give it to me."

"Well, first the good news. I trusted the sheriff and told him everything. I was allowed to keep my job. And just like you said, he understood the reasons why I held back on him. To protect my family."

"I'm glad to hear it. Now the bad news?"

"The bad news is also that I trusted the sheriff and told him everything. He asked me to set up a meeting with you that only would include him and us. But he was playing me for a fool. I overheard him in the hall after he thought I'd left the premises. The problem is that he doesn't trust you. There's a warrant out for your arrest. Did you know that?"

"No." Actually, he didn't. And now that things had ramped up, he could expect that the pressure to find him would increase.

"The sheriff planned on using me to meet with you and then arrest you. I think he's a good man, Quinn, under normal circumstances. It's just that he thinks that I can't see clearly because you have some kind of power over me. Those were his words, not mine."

"And what do you think?"

Incredulity edged her laugh. "I'll just have to prove them wrong, won't I? He thinks that arresting you will end the threats on me and my family."

He could only say he was sorry so many times. "Thanks for giving me the heads-up."

"I'm going to destroy this phone now. I'm not going to call you again. Don't come to the house, either. The bad guys are watching."

He pinched the bridge of his nose. She'd kept her job up to this point, sure, but this time, if the sheriff found out what she'd just done, she might not be so fortunate. "It's all right, Bree. I was about to call my superior. I didn't know there was a warrant for my arrest, but I'm going to turn myself in, if that's what it takes to end this."

"But if you were right about the dangers of being taken into custody, then you could end your life that way, too, Quinn. I won't stand by and let that happen."

"There's nothing you can do."

"Yes, there is. I can try to find out who is behind this. Expose them."

"No. Absolutely not. Right now it would be his word against mine, or I would have come forward sooner. But you are not to engage them in any way. I'm taking this out of your and your sheriff's hands by calling my superior. I'll end it my own way."

"Your own way?" A cynical huff came over the phone. "And I have no say in this at all? My life and Stevie's life are on the line until this is over. I can't just wait and do nothing. I didn't tell you but they only gave me twelve hours to turn you over to them. That means I have six hours left. And what did I do? I talked to the sheriff. That man said he was watching me, so it's likely he knows I went to my sheriff despite his warning."

"He knows that you're a deputy and have a job. There are a million things that could have taken you to the sheriff's department today. He doesn't know you told the sheriff." Yet.

Still, she hadn't told him before about the deadline. The clock was ticking. He needed to get off the phone with her and get this over with.

"Listen, Bree. I'm glad you called to tell me all this. I wouldn't hold it against your sheriff if he found and arrested me, but Sheriff Garrison is wrong about ending the threats. Since the money wasn't recovered, I fear retribution from these men. That means they could harm you or Stevie, whether or not I'm in jail." Or even whether or not he was alive. He ground his teeth. This got worse by the minute. He wished he could scoop her and Stevie up, and yeah, maybe even her dad, who detested him, and run away with them. "Listen, I want you to leave, Bree. You need to get away and hide. Go somewhere safe. Do you know anyone in Canada?"

"Quinn, you're scaring me."

"Good. I don't like where this is heading. Where are you now?"

"I'm in my car. I told the sheriff I was heading home to get breakfast, but I really just needed time to think, then I'll go back to the department. But with his deception, I don't know how to face him."

"Understandable. Here's what I want you to do. Don't even go home. Go directly to the airport and buy a ticket to anywhere."

"Are you crazy?"

"No. I'm completely sane. I want you to be safe. I'm going to walk right into the DEA office and sit in my superior's office with a witness or two, and tell them what I know. That will pull all the insanity away from Coldwater Bay, but it's going to take time for that to happen. I want you to be safe until then."

"Quinn, you won't make it there. You can't even get on a plane now. It would take you too long to drive there. Oh, wait. A call from Dad is coming through on my other phone. Can you wait a second?"

"Hurry." She should be heading to the airport. Why wouldn't she take him seriously?

"What?" Her voice came over the phone—but she wasn't talking to him. "No, Dad, no." The words came out in a wail.

TWELVE

Anguish engulfed Bree, but she focused enough to think clearly. To finish this conversation with Dad even though Stevie had been abducted. Kidnapped. The worst possible scenario. Exactly what she had tried to avoid.

She wanted to throw the phone and crumple. But she had to be strong for Stevie. For Dad. They never even made it on the plane before Stevie was taken.

Bree composed herself. Stopped the sniffles. "Dad, tell me everything."

"Now, listen carefully to me, Bree. You can't tell the sheriff. They warned me that if I called the police, I would never see my grandson again. I'm so, so sorry, Bree. I—" Sobs resounded through the phone.

She could hardly stand to hear her own father sobbing. "Dad. Daddy. Please, don't. We can't help Stevie if we fall apart. You have to pull yourself together."

"Okay. I'm sorry. I'm sorry," he said.

"It's okay. Now listen. Don't you blame yourself. You can't do that. But we have to get him back." She forced her voice to sound strong and determined, holding back the whimpers. "Nothing matters except getting him back." Not her. Not Dad. Not Quinn.

Only Stevie mattered. She would do anything. *Any-*

thing. To get him back here safely and deal with the consequences later. Deputy or not.

"Now, what are their demands?"

"He wants Quinn. Just like you told me early this morning. He wants Quinn in exchange for Stevie. Why did that jerk ever have to come back into our lives?" His anger boiled through their connection.

Bree would almost prefer his apologies to this. "Did the caller say anything else?"

"Yes. That you have six hours to find Quinn. He will contact you."

Right. The guy hadn't given her an extension on his deadline. Could be that he had his own deadline by which he had to deliver Quinn.

"Okay, Dad. It's going to be okay."

"I...don't know..." Her Dad's words were garbled with tears.

And the sound wrenched her through and through. "Dad, hold it together. You have to be strong for Stevie."

"Yes. I know. And for you. I just... I just can't lose—"

Steve's son. His only son's only son. His only grand-child.

"I know. And you're not going to. I've got this." What was she saying? She absolutely did not have this. She was grateful this call came through before she destroyed her only means to contact Quinn. She just hoped he was still on the other cell waiting for her.

"I keep thinking I should call the police, despite their warning. What do you want me to do?"

"Let me handle it on my end. You go to Idaho and stay there so I don't have to worry about you, too. For Stevie's sake, okay? You wait for them to call you. I'll let you know..."

"Know what, Bree? That you have Quinn and you're going to trade him?"

"Yes."

"You can't be serious."

She wished she wasn't. "Dad, please don't worry. It's going to work out fine."

How could she tell him things she wasn't so sure about? How could she reassure him like this? Maybe the reassurance was for her. She had to believe that Stevie would be all right, and that his Auntie Bree would save the day.

Her body quivered under the pressure.

"I know," he said. "I'll pray, that's all I can do. Pray for Stevie and for you. Bree…be careful." He ended the call before she could say more.

Oh, Lord, what am I going to do?

"Bree!"

She looked around. Where was that— Oh, she'd completely forgotten she had Quinn on the other phone.

"Yes, I'm here. I…" She sucked in a breath. "You heard?"

"Part of it. But not all of it. I'm assuming they took Stevie. Bree… There are no words." His anguished tone filtered through the cell.

He had to blame himself. Just like they all blamed themselves for their part in this. Dad, Bree and Quinn.

"I can't lose Stevie, too. Not Steve's little boy. Not my Stevie." She grappled with the unbearable pain, struggling to shove it aside enough to let her think clearly. Had to stay on top of this. If she lost it now, Stevie could die. But what could she do to save him?

Her options were limited.

"I'm not going to turn myself into the DEA, after all," Quinn said.

What? What was he saying? "Are you going to hide again, Quinn?" Disappointment suffused her.

"No." The one word was all it took for her to hear the hurt in his voice. "We're going to get him back," Quinn said. "I'm going to trade myself for Stevie."

He would do that? She could kick herself that her first thought had been to think the worst of him. Still, she couldn't allow this, despite what she'd told her dad. "No. Absolutely not. You can't. They'll kill you."

"Maybe. But getting Stevie back is all that matters, wouldn't you agree?"

Moments ago, she told herself she would do absolutely anything to get her nephew back. But trading another human being was off the table. "There has to be another way."

"Oh yeah, do you have any bright ideas?"

"Not yet, but I'm working on it. I can't lose Stevie, but neither can I lose you, Quinn. I won't give either of you up. Even to the sheriff I trusted." He'd used her. Maybe he'd had good intentions, but still, she wouldn't trust him with this.

What do I do, Lord?

Quinn's breath came in rasps over the line. "Listen to me closely, Bree. I worked undercover with these men for over a year. Nearly two. They're…brutal in ways I could never explain. I can't get the images out of my head. I don't want to scare you because now they have Stevie, but we can't mess around anymore. We can't waste a single second. You call your dad back and tell him you have me, and to set up the trade."

Her heart twisted so hard she thought it would rip apart. *I can't do that…*

"Quinn, you're asking too much. How can I do that? It isn't right. Please help me find another way."

But little Stevie was counting on her.

"I'm working on a plan. Will you trust me, Bree? You know I'd never do anything to harm Stevie. I'll do everything in my power to save him."

Yes, Bree believed him—because in that way, Quinn could possibly make up for his part in Steve's death. Steve had died in an accident, but Quinn was there and blamed himself for somehow not stopping it. She understood that completely because she felt the same way about herself.

She thought back to Quinn holding Steve in his arms as he stumbled all the way up on the beach, then collapsed on the sand. Quinn desperately wanted to save Stevie. And in this, she had no real choice but to trust him.

And she'd give him this, because he might just be giving his life for Stevie. "Yes, Quinn. I trust you."

"I'll be in touch," he said, and ended the call.

She stared at her cell, working up the nerve to call her father. Hyperventilating, she pressed her finger on his image on her phone. It rang, but he didn't answer. She left a voice mail.

"I've contacted Quinn. Set up the time and place to trade him for Stevie when he contacts you."

What am I doing?

Waiting for that call back from Bree with the information for the trade-off was pure torture.

Would she actually call and make the deal to trade him? He wasn't entirely sure. He half expected Sheriff Garrison to knock down his door and arrest him.

Nothing left for him to do except pace his room in the small run-down motel, close to town but with a low profile. He didn't care that it was a dump. It was just a place to hide until he had a way to get Stevie. A way for Quinn to get information to exonerate himself. In other words, a way to get back to working undercover. It could work both ways, and he could turn this blown cover and warrant for his arrest around to exonerate himself.

Time to make the call, only not to Bree.

Good thing he had a burner and another cell. He wouldn't have to use the cell that Bree would call him back on with the information about the trade for Stevie. Instead, he would call someone he hadn't trusted enough to call before, and for good reason.

An agent he knew well and had worked with on numerous occasions. She was smart and capable, but she was too by-the-book to work well with him. He could never trust her to secrecy because she wouldn't bend the rules or jeopardize her job. She was black-and-white, despite working in an arena where everything was black and gray.

Except this time, she was the only person he could call. He could only hope and pray that she would be willing to bend this time because a little boy's life was at stake.

He pushed the numbers into the cell, hoping he could still reach her at the same number.

After a few rings a woman answered. "Agent McKesson speaking."

"Hi, Julia."

A gasp came over the cell. "Qui-Quinn." Then, she whispered. "Agent Strand?"

Former Agent Strand. Ex-agent. Right now I feel more like a fugitive.

"Yes."

"I don't understand. After all this time, you call *me*? What's going on?"

She could be putting him on speakerphone even now and signaling the rest of them to listen in and trace the call for all he knew. She could mislead him in order to bring him in, just like Sheriff Garrison had done to Bree. But Quinn knew her weakness. And he was about to use it. He would cut right to the heart of the matter.

"I don't care about *my* life, Julia." He barely cared about justice at this particular moment. He just wanted Stevie back where he belonged. "A little boy's life is in danger, and I need your help. Can I trust you?"

"Well, that depends."

Figured.

"On what?"

"You. I won't get involved in anything illegal. Quinn, you must know there's a warrant for your arrest."

"I know that I've been set up. Now someone has been abducted." He drew in a breath, then, "Julia. He's only five."

Oh, now he was just being cruel. Julia had lost her little boy—he'd been only three—to a stray bullet from gangbangers working with DTOs—drug trafficking organizations. They had kidnapped her son to get at her husband. Both her son and husband had been killed in the cross fire.

She gasped. He could picture her frowning and angry with him. She knew exactly what he was doing.

"Let me guess. They want you in exchange for the boy."

"Yes. And I'm going to give them what they want."

"I'm assuming you haven't called the authorities."

"I have. I'm calling you."

"You know I have to turn you over. I have to turn this over—"

"A boy's life is hanging in the balance. Those creeps

have him. Julia… You know how this can turn out."
Please, God, let me reach her. Quinn realized he hadn't
been praying nearly enough, but maybe he shouldn't
wait until he was utterly desperate.

"I do. And let me be perfectly clear, I see what's
going on here. I know what you're trying to do to me,
and I do not appreciate it."

"Does that mean you're going to help me?"

A sigh over the phone, then, "Yes, I'll help you. Tell
me what you need from me."

Quinn laid out his plan, fully aware that she could
turn him in to the DEA or she could turn him in to Michael Jones. He'd been hiding from both the good guys
and the bad guys. But Julia had never been a double-
crosser. She'd never been a liar. If she said she would
help, he believed her.

And together, Quinn, Bree and Julia would get Stevie back.

And he would find convincing evidence to bring
Declan down.

Three hours later, Quinn still paced the suffocat-
ing room. They were running out of time. Bree had already called him back with the time and place for the
trade here in Coldwater Bay. They had less than forty-
five minutes.

Come on, Julia.

He wasn't sure if law enforcement would break down
his door or if a hit man would find him here. He didn't
like to be confined to a place without a backdoor escape,
but leaving the premises could jeopardize him as well.

He was at the mercy of just about everyone at this
moment, a position he never wanted to be in. Well, except for God—he could use God's mercy.

He stared at the bed and the floor. For once in his life, he should probably drop to his knees and pray like his mother used to do. He would find her on her knees praying in the middle of the night. Pain pricked his heart. He didn't have time to think about the past, and the fact that maybe he'd been angry with God his entire life. Why had Mom and Dad died in that accident? Such a cruel fate for such wonderful people.

He frowned, unwilling and unready to let it all go.

A soft knock came at the door. He readied his weapon and peered through the peephole, fully aware these could be his last seconds of life.

Julia.

He cracked the door enough for her to slip inside.

"You're here." Finally.

She shrugged and acted as if she might hug him, then thought better of it. "Sorry it took me so long. I couldn't exactly wait for the next commercial flight and get here in time, so I called in a favor from a friend with a private jet."

He breathed easier. She'd gone to a lot of trouble. "Thank you."

She eyed him up and down. "You look like a wreck."

"Get used to seeing me like this. I'll be a wreck until Stevie is back."

"What about you, Quinn? What do you think is going to happen to you?"

"Well, if my plan succeeds, I'll be exonerated."

"Why did it have to come to this? You could have come in sooner."

"Come on, Julia. You might live by the book, but there are others who don't, and you know that. I needed to find out more. Find evidence, solid evidence, so it wouldn't be my word against his. I didn't steal the money."

He'd holed up in the camper, but come down the mountain to gather intel, research on the internet and find out what he could, which hadn't been much. His hands had been tied by his limited access to resources. All he could do was wait for things to die down, and the truth about Declan would come out on its own. Declan could blow his own cover and his double-crossing without Quinn around to blame. Or Michael could find out it had been Declan who stole the money.

Sometimes it was best to wait things out.

He suddenly realized Julia was staring. He'd been lost in thought.

The way she eyed him, he could see that she wasn't sure she trusted him.

"Why are you helping me if you think I'm guilty?"

"I didn't say that I think you're guilty. But you convinced me to help you because of the boy. Now let's focus on getting him back."

He nodded. "Right. You're right. Thank you, again." He couldn't really thank her enough. "I owe you."

"Like you're going to be able to repay," she said.

Because he would be dead. *Come on, Julia, have a little faith.*

He pulled a chair out for her at the small round table. She took a seat and he sat opposite her.

"Just stick to the plan we discussed. Did you bring it?"

She rolled her eyes and sighed. "Sure. You know it's a prototype, right? I had to call in another favor."

He grinned. "That's what I like about you, Julia. You have a lot of connections."

Her eyes widened. "And some connections with

some unsavory characters." She batted her fake lashes, her way of letting him know she referred to him.

Except he wasn't unsavory. Far from it. This situation had made him out to be just that, though.

"Time to get down to business." She opened up her bag and pulled out a box. "Roll up your sleeve, please."

He did as she asked. She swabbed his upper arm with an alcohol wipe, then pulled out a huge needle.

Whoa, whoa... "Wait a minute."

"Scared of needles, are we?"

"Well, you gotta admit, that's a monster."

"How else are we going to inject you with this tracking microchip?"

"Are you sure this is safe?"

"No. You asked for it."

Yes. Yes, he did.

She pressed the large needle against his skin, then blinked her big eyes up at him. "Let me be clear that I don't like your plan." Then she plunged the needle in and injected the microchip.

He gritted his teeth. He sure hoped this would work, because he was at the very least betting his life on it.

"If you knew what I'd been through already, you'd understand why I'm willing to hand myself over to them." He'd been tortured before. "While I'd prefer not to go through it again, knowing that someone has my back can get me through."

"So, what? You'll let them torture you and then you'll tell them where the money is?"

"Come on, you don't think I took it."

"I don't know what to think. But I'm in this with you now. So you'd better find a way to exonerate yourself."

"With your help, maybe I can."

"That's why I'm here. Now let's go get the boy."

She drove him over to Bree's house in her rental car and parked down the street. He got out, then peered at her through the window. "You have the address. Just stick to the plan."

THIRTEEN

Quinn entered through the back door of Bree's house. In the living room, she whipped around, her red hair flying, her face twisted in anguish.

Before he could say a word, she laid into him. "You're late, Quinn! We're running out of time."

"We have plenty of time."

"The sheriff is probably watching me. The bad guys could be watching, too. If anyone arrests you then Stevie could lose his life. If the man behind the kidnapping gets his hands on you without my help, then why would he bother giving me Stevie?"

She was losing it. He didn't blame her and understood—he felt like crumbling, too. Poor Bree. He closed the distance, then as he lifted his hand, she flinched. He thought better of reaching out to comfort her.

Instead he scraped a hand down his face again—it was becoming a habit. Was he risking too much by coming here? All of what she said could be true, except… "Nobody saw me. I made sure nobody was watching."

She pressed her hands to her face. Quinn didn't let himself reason through the whys or why nots. He rushed to embrace her. He held her tight.

A few minutes later, her tears spent, she stepped away and stared at him. Terror was clearly gripping her.

"We have to go now, Bree. Come on, you can do this."

"No, I can't do this. I can't exchange you. It has nothing to do with my job as a deputy."

He grabbed her hands. "I carried Steve to you. I'll never get over that. But let me do this. Let me give you Stevie. Get him back for you. Besides, you don't have a choice. I'm going there with or without you. You're not handing me over. I'm delivering myself."

"I have to be there, too—for Stevie. I have to go so I can make sure he's all right."

Though Quinn didn't like the idea of Bree being there at all, Stevie needed her to be there for the exchange. Julia would only be there as backup to protect both Stevie and Bree. No one would know she was there, not even Bree.

"Okay, then, so what are we waiting on?" he asked.

She dangled keys. "I borrowed my neighbor's car for this afternoon, just to throw off anyone who might follow me in my car. The sheriff is hoping I'll meet up with you, after all. I know he asked me to tell him before it happens and made a show of trusting me to do that, but…"

"You don't believe he'll trust you."

"Not as far as he can throw me, because he thinks I'm under your influence." She emphasized the word with finger quotes. "The only influence I'm under is the deep need to save Stevie. If working with you is what it takes, then so be it. My job doesn't matter anymore."

Yeah, working with the unsavory Quinn, as Julia had called him, had to give them both a bad reputation. He blew out a breath. Now, to turn it all upside down.

Driving Bree's neighbor's old white sedan, he steered them out of the quiet neighborhood, going the long way around so they wouldn't pass through town, and out to the bay area, toward their destination. With ten minutes to spare, he found the rutted drive out to Coldwater Bay where an old run-down oyster factory sat, long ago replaced with a newfangled building a few miles away. What a waste of property. This part of the bay was in serious need of a beautification project.

As the sedan bounced along the uneven road, he looked for signs of an unwanted law enforcement detail, or of Julia. He hoped he saw neither but for different reasons.

"You didn't call him, did you?"

"Who? The sheriff? Of course not. All I care about right now is Stevie."

"Same here."

In a few short minutes, Stevie could be safe with Bree. And Quinn could be drawn and quartered. He'd actually seen these guys do that. He hadn't been able to stop it.

His heart hammered at the thought of what he was about to face.

There's no other way...

He pulled the car to the side of the road just about fifteen yards out from where the warehouse sat along the water. The sky was blue and partly cloudy. Seagulls hovered on the wind and danced in the air, like it was just another day.

And it was—for everyone except for Bree, Stevie and Quinn. He reached for the door handle and made to get out.

She touched his arm. "Wait, Quinn. I don't know what to expect. How will I handle Stevie? What do I tell him? He must be scared to death."

"My guess is that he won't remember a thing."

"What?"

"They will have probably drugged him."

Her face paled.

"That way he won't remember faces or names. It's better that way, Bree. You don't want him to remember the horror of being kidnapped and held for ransom."

Her head bobbed up and down as if in agreement. "I didn't mean that, Quinn. What I said earlier. I didn't mean that all I care about right now is Stevie."

"It's okay. Stevie is all we should care about. Getting him back and keeping him safe."

"I care about you." She grabbed his hand as if she wouldn't let him go. Her hand trembled in his. "Are you sure about this?"

"Yes. Stick to the plan. Stay strong, for Stevie. Once you have him take him away from here. Don't pass go. Don't collect two hundred dollars. Don't look back. Don't come back for me. I have a plan and I'll be in touch."

She eased closer and grabbed his collar, pulling him to her. Bree pressed her lips to his in a quick kiss. "Stay alive, Quinn Strand."

"That's the plan." Though he hadn't told her the whole of it.

He wished she hadn't kissed him because that messed with his head. He had to focus on the dangerous, deadly task ahead of him with a child's life at stake. Instead, all he could think about was the softness of her lips on his.

Ears roaring with his skyrocketing pulse, he opened the car door and made his way to the warehouse, one grueling footstep after another. Images of fighting his way through the thugs to get Stevie ran through his brain. What if he could do this that way? Strong-arm his way through a wall of armed and dangerous thugs to rescue one little boy.

All of his ideas were too risky for Stevie. One stray bullet and he could end up just like Julia's son.

One thing he knew, Michael kept his word. When he told his men he would kill them if they didn't return with Quinn, they believed him. When he told his men to exchange Stevie for Quinn, they would hand the boy over. Unharmed. Untouched.

And in return, as Michael envisioned it, Quinn would hand over the money.

That was all it was ever about.

The love of money was the root of all evil. His mom used to tell him that scripture from the Bible. After what he had seen, he knew that to be 100 percent true. And evil men fed off others, pushing drugs to hook the weak into a lifelong addiction, all for more money, until hundreds of millions of dollars sat wrapped in plastic, filling warehouses.

Agent Declan Miller hadn't thought Michael Jones would miss a few hundred grand. But Michael had, and Quinn had been set up to take the fall.

Three men rushed to surround him, pointing fully automatic guns at his chest.

Bree blinked her eyes open. Grogginess clung to her. "What—"

She sensed someone…a presence… Quinn? Bree twisted around on the sofa to see a strange woman sitting in a chair.

She bolted upright. Pain throbbed through her temples. Bree reached for her weapon. Where was it?

"Relax." The woman held up her badge.

"DEA?" She must be here for Quinn. "I don't—"

"Just wait, and I'll explain. Stevie is here. He's in the bed."

"Stevie!" Bree got up and rushed to his room. She cradled him in her arms. The woman followed.

"I don't understand. What's happened?" She couldn't remember anything. She and Quinn had gone to meet the men to get Stevie back. To trade him for Stevie. What had she done? Why had she agreed to it?

"He's not waking up. What's the matter with him?"

"He is going to be fine. I suspect they gave him something to knock him out so he wouldn't see their faces. The same as they gave you so you couldn't share with the police the faces of all the men involved in the kidnapping. Drugging you saved both your lives."

Except Bree had already seen some of their faces that day on the river. Maybe those men were expendable in the organization.

Bree lowered little Stevie to the pillow. He was so pale. "Come on, sweetie. Wake up." She turned toward the other woman. "I should get him to the ER just to make sure."

His eyes blinked open. "Auntie Bree?" His words sounded groggy, just like she felt.

She squeezed him to her again, never wanting to let him go.

Thank You, Lord! He was here safe and sound with her at home. "It's okay, honey." She settled him back on the bed and ran her fingers over his forehead, brushing back his hair. "Just rest now."

His eyelids fluttered until they closed again. "Sleep, sweetie. Sleep." But she really wanted him to wake up and be himself again. She pressed her hands over her eyes. What was going on? Why couldn't she remember? She'd watched Quinn walking forward.

But nothing after that. She remembered nothing. Did this woman have anything to do with that? She twisted her head to look up at the woman, delivering a glare.

The woman had long black hair and dark brown eyes. A beauty, really. The agent offered a tenuous smile. "You're the woman in the picture."

Bree scrunched up her face, irritated at this intruder in her home, DEA or not. "What picture?"

"Quinn always carries a picture of a woman with him. It's you."

Bree had no idea what to think. "I don't see what that has to do with anything. What is it that you want?"

"Look, Bree...may I call you that?"

Bree pushed up from Stevie's bed and watched him. How long before he was back to normal? "Sure, and you said your name was—"

"I didn't. Can we talk? Leave him to sleep?"

Though she didn't want to leave Stevie alone, she nodded her agreement and bent down to kiss him on the cheek, whispering, "I'll be back. You sleep."

His eyes popped open, surprising Bree. "I want Grandpa."

"Grandpa will be here soon." She'd have to call him to let him know what had happened. "Now rest, sweetie. I'll make you a smoothie in a little while, okay?"

He smiled, then rolled over. Her heart leaped.

She closed Stevie's door, wanting nothing more than to take him away from here. Take him away from anyone who wanted to harm him. Anyone who would ever try to snatch him again. Bree followed the woman through the house, stopping momentarily to grab a hidden weapon. She wanted protection in case she needed it.

Once they were in the living area, the woman turned,

her expression somber. "I'm Agent Julia McKesson. We have a problem."

"No kidding. What has happened? I—"

"I brought you both back here. The men, well...they drugged you. You were sitting in the car and they came up behind you. You fought them. You obviously don't remember that part."

No. She didn't. "And you know this how?"

"I was watching everything. Quinn traded himself for the boy. They left you and the boy—"

"It's Stevie."

"Stevie. They left you and Stevie in the car sleeping. After they were gone, I brought you both back here. Quinn recruited me to be a hidden backup to protect the two of you. And I've done that. But it's Quinn I'm worried about now."

Bree eased onto the sofa. *Oh, Lord, what have we done? Please protect him.* "You're DEA. Why did you let him do this?"

"You're a deputy. Why did you?"

"I don't know. I... I couldn't let them hurt Stevie."

"Neither could Quinn. Neither could I."

"What now? He told me that he had a plan. He made me believe it was the only way, and that he would make it work." She pressed her hands over her face. "What have I done?"

"You got your son back."

"He's my nephew."

"Whatever. You have the child back, so you can't blame yourself. I'm not sure how much he shared with you, but Quinn *does* have a plan. The problem is that I'm going to need your help."

"Why is that a problem?"

"Quinn didn't want you in on this."

"I don't get it. Why didn't he share his plan with me?"

"He was trying to protect you."

"But you're not."

"I'm trying to get Quinn back."

"Do you love him?" She could see the two of them to-gether. Handsome Quinn and beautiful Julia. They were both DEA. Quinn had called her in to help him. Had trusted her with his plan. He'd trusted Julia and not Bree.

The woman laughed. "I couldn't love a man who was always looking at another woman's picture."

Point taken. Bree wasn't sure how she felt about Quinn looking at her picture, but she'd ponder that an-other time. His life was in danger now.

A noise at the door brought Bree to her feet with her weapon. Agent McKesson, too.

Dad stumbled into the house and his eyes grew wide. He immediately threw up his hands.

Bree dropped her weapon. "Dad!" She rushed to him. Hugged him. "What are you doing here?"

"Someone contacted me and told me to come home to help you and Stevie." Her father's eyes shifted to something over her shoulder.

"Grandpa!" Stevie ran to him and jumped in his arms.

"Hey, little buddy. I'm so sorry we didn't get to make our trip."

"Dad, you should go to Idaho with Stevie. This isn't over. Please."

"This time, we'll escort you and make sure you get on that plane," Julia said. "Make sure your relatives meet you at the airport."

Dad's eyes cut to the other woman in the room. "And you are?"

"She's with the DEA. She is helping Quinn."

"I'm the one who contacted you, per Quinn's instructions," she said.

Dad eyed her as he put Stevie down. "Can you do me a favor, buddy? Can you go get yourself a glass of milk and wait for me in the kitchen?"

Stevie nodded and ran between them to the kitchen.

Dad leveled his gaze on her. She was a little girl again, being scolded. "You were told not to involve the police. You could have lost Stevie forever, Bree. That was a huge risk. I counted on you."

"Your father doesn't trust the police?" Julia asked.

"Those were the demands." Bree paced the small space, wanting to get away from the tension and go find Quinn.

"And you trust her because..." her father said.

"I brought your daughter and grandson back here to the house after the abductors left them unconscious in a car. They had drugged them so they wouldn't have to kill them."

Dad threw his hands up in the air, a show of exasperation. "Well, that's comforting."

"We don't have time to talk about this, Dad. Now, are you going to take Stevie away from here or not?"

"Sure. And just so you know, I might not bring him back."

Great way to encourage me, Dad. He was understandably upset about all of this. But she totally got where he was coming from. She might feel the same way if she were in his shoes, though she knew he would never take Stevie away from her.

"Can we get on with it?" Julia said. "Every minute we stand here talking is a minute we're wasting. Quinn's life depends on us."

FOURTEEN

Pain rolled through him as he moved in and out of consciousness. He had to stay awake. How long had he been in this condition? When darkness started to take him under again, Quinn pulled himself out of it.

Focused on staying conscious. Pictured Bree's face. Imagined her telling him to stay awake. To make it out alive. He recalled those last few moments with her. She'd grabbed him and kissed him.

Stay alive, Quinn Strand. He could hear her sweet voice in his head now.

He'd told her that staying alive was the plan. Problem was, he struggled to remember exactly how he planned to stay alive, or if there had been any real plan at all beyond saving Stevie. He'd watched the boy be delivered to her in the car. But that's all he'd seen before he'd been whisked away into the warehouse. Then whisked away again.

So he had no idea where he was.

He was alone at the moment, having given them what they wanted, but he'd taken a lot of abuse, not wanting to give the information up too soon.

He'd wanted to give Bree the time she needed to get Stevie somewhere safe. He was actually surprised they didn't offer to trade Stevie for the money instead of Quinn, but it seemed that they wanted him either way and believed they could, through torture, force him to tell them where he'd hidden it.

He had to make them work for it, and eventually, he'd given them a bogus location.

Water dripped incessantly, echoing through the dampness. Another warehouse? He couldn't be sure. There was a bag over his head; he couldn't see where he was. He wouldn't be able to see out of his left eye, even if he didn't have a bag over his head. They had transported him to another location away from the oyster warehouse along that part of Coldwater Bay. The drive had taken maybe half an hour but he couldn't be sure, because he'd been kicked in the head a few times. He hoped he could remember his name when he came out of this.

When being the operative word.

The worst pain came from his pinkie finger, which wouldn't stop throbbing, protesting the violence inflicted upon it. He'd held out as long as he could, so they would believe him about the money. When they'd started on the pinkie fingernail, he spilled his guts. But he'd managed to get information out of them, too— whether they'd realized that was what he was doing or not.

He'd gotten the confirmation he'd needed. Heard the name he'd wanted to hear—Declan had been the one to tell them he had seen Quinn taking money. A complete lie to divert attention from himself. Declan had also told them Quinn was undercover DEA. Unfortunately, these guys were especially brutal to him because they knew he was DEA. Quinn was surprised they didn't kill him.

But they had to find the money. If it wasn't there, then he was dead. And if it *was* there, then he was probably dead, too. He wouldn't put it past Declan at this point to plant the money somewhere, setting Quinn up, so Declan would be off the hook. Except Quinn suspected the man had already spent the original stolen money.

That had been the risky part of the plan. Quinn hadn't stolen the money so he couldn't tell them where it was hidden. He'd fabricated a location in order to stop the questioning and get them all to leave. But if he was still here when they got back, his pinkie finger would be the last of his worries.

Others would suffer, too.

Bree and Stevie...

Okay, he had to get out of here. *Focus, man. Focus.* He shook off the agony of the last several hours. He started shaking his chair, bouncing hard on it in order to break it.

Footsteps told him he wasn't alone.

Not good. He couldn't get out of this with a guard watching over him. And by the boots clomping along the concrete, he could tell the guard was approaching him.

Moments later, he could smell the sweaty man in front of him. "Shut up or I'll make you shut up."

"But I haven't said anything." Quinn would have to appease him.

"You were moving around. And now you're talking."

Quinn stilled as if to obey. He hoped it was enough. He envisioned the man coldcocking him with the butt of his gun. Quinn sucked in a breath to brace himself. He could get knocked unconscious again and wake up to more torture over the money he didn't have.

Now what?

Come on, Julia. What's taking so long?

They hadn't discovered his tracker, so she should have found him by now.

Gunfire resounded.

Not machine guns.

Julia. He hoped.

Grunts and kicks met his ears. Someone engaged the guy guarding him. The bag was yanked from his head. Pain thundered through his temples. "Ow!"

He opened his one good eye.

A beautiful woman with burning green eyes and fiery red hair stared down at him.

"Bree," he croaked out. "What are you doing here?"

"Saving you, what do you think?" She eyed him, a look of horror on her face. That and relief. Bree hugged him.

The slightest of touches was painful, but he wouldn't tell her that.

"Thank you for getting Stevie back," she said.

"No time for that. You can kiss and make up later." Julia said. "We're running behind."

Bree cut him from the chair, and the women shouldered him out of the dilapidated structure. "It's okay," he protested. "I'm good to walk."

"No, you're not," they said in unison.

He lay in the back of Julia's rental car as Julia explained all that had happened. She'd done as he'd asked and protected Bree.

"Get us back to Bree's house."

"You should be prepared to be threatened again. Maybe the two of you should just leave, too, like your father did with Stevie."

"And go where?" Bree said. "I'm not leaving my home. I won't go into hiding like Quinn did...sorry, Quinn. No offense."

"None taken." Or at least he didn't think so. *Wait a minute...*

"I'm not taking you back to your house. That's too dangerous—Jones and his men know where it is. We'll just go back to the seedy motel where Quinn still has a room."

Good. He wasn't thinking clearly. Julia was right.

"What I mean is that I have family and loved ones. People I want to see. I can't hide in the mountains in a camper until this dies down."

Ouch. "You're cutting me to the bone here, Bree. I thought I was already beaten up enough." It was clear that she hadn't fully understood his reasons for his actions.

She tossed a glance over her shoulder at him in the back seat. "I just thought it was time for truth instead of always dancing around things."

What? Dancing around things? What was she talking about?

"That's a smart girlfriend you have there, Quinn." Julia steered them through downtown. He hoped they didn't get pulled over.

"I'm not his girlfriend," Bree said.

"Whatever you say," Julia chuckled. She cleared her throat. "Okay, let's talk about what's next. I need to get on my cell if I can't be there in person. Maybe I can convince Stan that Declan is involved—that he blew your cover and has framed you for stolen money."

"That's not going to work without proof. Jones's men have probably already discovered there's no money in that location by now. So I have to come up with a new plan."

"Just tell Jones it's Declan who knows where the

money is," Julia said. "That he framed you. Set you up. They torture him, I guarantee he'll tell them."

"And he's going to believe me now, why?"

"Because I'm going to tell him." Julia sounded smug.

"I know I'm not DEA here," Bree said, "and I don't do things the way you do, but how does that make you any better than this Declan agent? If you're just going to put his life in danger."

"Good point." Julia sighed. "I'm not above turning this back on the man who is to blame. But it would be better if DEA arrested him rather than him disappearing into some torture chamber. But for that we need proof."

"What we need is a confession," Quinn said.

"You're never going to get that."

Julia wasn't kidding. This was a seedy motel room. A good hiding place, too. Her only immediate concern was infection. This place was probably crawling with germs and definitely wasn't the best place to give Quinn first aid—doctor his wounds and scratches. She could hardly bear to look at him.

The thought of what he'd gone through made her physically ill, but she wouldn't let him see that and forced a tenuous smile to her face. Relaxed the lines she knew tried to inch between her brows and across her forehead.

"Just hold still," Bree said. "I wish we could just take you to the doctor instead of this nasty motel. You could get a secondary infection here."

He made a weird sound, almost like he tried to laugh but pain prevented him. "Secondary infections are common in hospitals. Ever heard of—" A racking cough cut him off.

"Careful now. Don't try to talk."

That cough worried her. She'd looked at his ribs, but none were broken. As a deputy, she had some basic medical training, and all that training was telling her now to get him to a qualified, experienced doctor, which she was not.

She'd put ice on his swollen eye. Maybe a raw steak would be better.

She'd doctored his face.

Bandaged his fingers, taking special care with the pinkie from which his fingernail had been stripped. *Hold it together.* She blew out a breath to keep her hands steady and focused on a particularly nasty cut along his arm.

While she cleaned, she focused on something other than Quinn's blood. Julia had gone to grab fast food. For the first time since this nightmare had started, Bree could finally relax—if only a little. Dad and Stevie were safe in Idaho. Quinn was safe here with her. Nobody was actively chasing them at this moment. Nobody was shooting at them.

Perspectives could sure change on the turn of a dime, Dad always said.

She thought about how she had braced herself to find Quinn in the warehouse, fearing what she would see. And here she was, tending to his wounds. She struggled to swallow against the sudden thickness in her throat.

"I'm sorry, Quinn," she whispered. "I can't believe you would go through this when you knew this was going to happen."

He released a grunt and nothing more as she continued to administer first aid.

"You're good at this, you know?" His one good eye peeked at her.

"At what?"

"At nurturing. But that doesn't surprise me in the least. You could have been a doctor or a nurse. Anything you wanted. Why did you choose to be a deputy?"

"I could ask you the same. Why did you go into the DEA?" *And put yourself in this kind of dangerous path?*

"I guess if I hadn't, we wouldn't be here now in this situation."

What could she possibly say to that? She bandaged the wound. "I'm afraid you could have a concussion. I definitely think there's internal bleeding based on the way your torso is bruised."

"I'm fine. I've been through worse."

Bree glared at him. Maybe that look she always gave Stevie when she expected a different response would work on Quinn—though she doubted it.

"Look, I promise to seek medical treatment when this is over. Happy?"

Wow. That had worked. She'd have to remember that next time. "Well, if that's the best I can get from you, it will have to do."

She packed away the first aid kit and threw away the blood-soaked gauze, then washed her hands, trying to ignore the stained sink.

Would this ever be over? She hoped so, but right now it was hard to see the end. She turned around. Quinn still sat in that same chair with his eyes closed.

Sleeping or just resting? He had refused painkillers. She slowly approached until she felt the heat coming off him. His metabolism had ramped up. His body trying to heal?

"If we had called the police once Stevie was taken," she said, "maybe you wouldn't have had to go through this."

"Maybe I'd be dead. Maybe Stevie, too."

She'd wanted to quit dancing around the issues and

speak the truth, but she had a hard time telling him what she really thought. Still, she had to try. "I didn't call the police when Stevie was abducted because I believed you about that being more dangerous for him. But the way things stand now, maybe that would have been the better way to go. You wouldn't have almost lost your life. You wouldn't be suffering now."

She moved to step away.

His eye flew open and he caught her wrist. "Nothing has turned out the way I thought it would."

The way he looked at her now, with longing and regret, made her think of their kiss in the garage. Was he referring to her, too? Not just everything that had happened so far with his being framed?

"Quinn, I…"

He reached up and brushed a knuckle down her face, apparently oblivious to the bruises that remained from his last few days of trying to survive and escape the madness. She pressed her hand over his on her cheek and squeezed.

"Thank you for what you did. For saving Stevie. But I don't want you to put yourself in that position again."

"There aren't any guarantees. You're still in danger." He slowly eased from the chair and leaned too far to the right. He supported himself on the chair. The tenderness in his face had fled and was replaced by anger.

"You should distance yourself from me in every way. I'm a train wreck right now. I thought I could protect you, but I don't know how anymore. You should leave."

"What do you mean? Leave you here injured like this?"

He nodded. "This isn't your fight. It never was." He released the chair and reached for her then, gently pulling her to him.

Her whole body shook. "Even if you hadn't been

there in the woods, I'd be fighting these men. They wanted me dead before you got involved."

"They let you go because of me. You traded me. I only thought to get Stevie back and gain intel. Now that we're on the other side of that operation, I see that nothing has changed nor will it change until I end this once and for all. But for the moment, Bree, you're still in danger."

He released her and she wished he hadn't. She didn't want to be afraid again.

"And Bree—" he looked at her, his eye fierce under his brow "—you're a good deputy. The best. I'm sorry for the trouble I've caused you."

She was the one to grab him this time. She gripped his shoulders and made him face her. "You saved Stevie. That's all that matters. Now let me help you. Let me protect you."

"I don't want you to lose your job because of me."

"Don't worry. I won't."

Bree gently hugged him. Somehow, they had to make it through this, and on the other side, she would have to let Quinn go again. She wouldn't let herself love him. There was no time for that, even if she could fall for him a third time, but when he left again—and he would; he always did—it would hurt her just like always.

Quinn eased her away from him and headed for the mirror to look at the damage.

The door burst open. "Police! Freeze!"

FIFTEEN

His arms clasped behind his head, Quinn stared at the ceiling in the county jail cell. For the first time since he'd been betrayed, he almost wanted to give up. He certainly hadn't imagined himself here in the small cell in a small town in Coldwater Bay. Betrayed by none other than his old flame.

Bree had called the cops on him.

I don't want you to lose your job because of me.

Don't worry. I won't.

Now her words made a lot more sense. What an idiot he'd been!

He squeezed his good eye shut and relived the moment when Bree betrayed him.

The door kicked in. Quinn's reflexes were slow, but he'd turned, preparing to protect her.

Two deputies pointed weapons at him. "Police! Freeze!"

Shock rolled through him.

Sheriff Garrison came in behind them. "Good work, Deputy Carrington."

Good work, Deputy Carrington? Bree?

The words sliced his heart up and fed it to the wolves.

Quinn whipped his head around to her. His blood

pressure spiked, sending blood bursting through his veins, oozing from the bandages, pounding through his head.

She looked as shell-shocked as he felt. Her mouth opened to speak, but no words came out as she shook her head slowly. What was that look in her eyes? Regret that she'd been caught?

"You called the cops on me?"

He didn't wait for her reply and instead hung his head. He couldn't look at her. He wouldn't look Bree Carrington in the eye. Maybe not ever again. He thought she understood what he was up against, especially since Julia was working with them to get at Declan. But Bree had Stevie back, and now she wanted to keep her job.

He didn't blame her. How could he?

Still, when she was in danger, and Stevie, too, Quinn had been willing to give his life. He thought that might have earned him at least a little loyalty in return.

In the parking lot in front of God and everybody, his wrists were cuffed, and he was ushered over to the sheriff's county vehicle and forced into the back seat.

Humiliated. Betrayed. He could only blame himself. He'd been the one under a spell—Bree's spell. She was beautiful inside and out. Mesmerizing. He had never truly gotten over her. And that had been his biggest mistake.

In his peripheral vision he could see her red hair spilling over her shoulders. His chest felt like it had a hole in it. How had he let her in like that? He thought he'd guarded himself better. He forced his eyes up, looking at anything but Bree, careful not to telegraph that he was looking for someone.

Somewhere in the parking lot, Julia was probably driving up with their fast food. When she saw what was happening, she would hang back for the time being to regroup and figure out what to do next. No sense in her landing behind bars, too, just from her association with him. No telling what Bree would tell them. Maybe Bree had called the police because she truly thought Quinn would be better protected. Regardless, he wished he hadn't involved Julia. She could also be in danger, but she was a completely capable agent, and now…his only hope.

He made the mistake of looking out the window and caught sight of Bree standing in a group of deputies, flashing blue and red lights painting colors over them. She glanced his way and caught his eye, her gaze pleading, her head subtly shaking.

Smart move, Bree.

He hadn't seen it coming.

Just like he hadn't seen it coming with Declan— who'd framed him. He hadn't actually thought the guy would go that far.

Groaning, he shoved thoughts of the deputies bursting through the door to arrest him to the far shelf in his mind. It only infuriated him. Tired of counting the old tiles on the ceiling, Quinn rolled to his side. Pain jarred him, the hard cot an insult to his body as he turned. He should insist they take him to the hospital, but he didn't have the energy right now. And truthfully, in his current predicament, he was safer here than in a hospital. Might as well get some sleep until the next round. He needed to rest and heal and figure out how he would take down Declan.

Except he couldn't sleep.

God, why have You abandoned me?

Or maybe it was Quinn who'd abandoned God when his parents died. And then every tragedy after that seemed to push him further away. Still, that day he'd seen Bree on the boat and the men had shot her, Quinn had begged God to protect her. To let Quinn reach her in time.

And he had.

Thank You...

Two sets of boots with a purposeful stride warned him of incoming enemy fire, heading his way. He should get up and face this, but he remained where he lay. Several other inmates took up cells in the small county jail. Maybe the incoming fire was for them and not him.

But keys jangled at Quinn's cell door. He rolled over and sat on the edge of his cot before he was made to sit up. He couldn't take any more bruises or torture, but he reminded himself this was the county jail. He wouldn't be tortured here. The sheriff was a good man and just doing his job, even though he was seeing things from his own narrow perspective.

With his good eye he watched Deputy Woodbridge unlock the cell. Another man stood next to him.

"Quinn Strand."

Quinn stood to his feet. "Who are you?"

"Agent Shepherd." The man flashed a badge. DEA. "What? Don't recognize it?" Sarcasm laced Agent Shepherd's tone.

Oh, great. One of those.

"Hold your wrists out, please."

Quinn did as he was asked, hating every second of his loss of freedom. The deputy cuffed him. "You're going with Shepherd here."

The sense of foreboding filled his gut. "Is that right?"

Shepherd shoved him out the door. He almost collapsed but fell against the bars and hung on.

"Easy now," the deputy said. "Strand's been through a beating. Can't you see?"

"Then why isn't he in the hospital?"

The deputy didn't respond to Shepherd's question, because it was more rhetorical, and the deputy seemed a tad intimidated by Shepherd. Understandable. He led them down the long hallway, Quinn's squeaky sneakers joining the clomping boots. The deputy opened a side door to reveal a vehicle parked and waiting, presumably Shepherd's.

Quinn didn't exit. "Deputy Woodbridge, I prefer to stay in the county jail. I don't believe Shepherd is who he claims to be."

"Good one, Quinn," Woodbridge said. "You just keep trying."

Quinn wasn't going to go through the door so easily. "Call the DEA. Call Stan Rollins, my superior. Check this man's credentials. Do that before you send me with him, please."

"He has the authorization papers in order for the transfer." Still, Deputy Woodbridge looked between the two men.

Shepherd sent the deputy a condescending look. "You really are a country bumpkin if you're going to let this guy fool you."

"Go on, Strand. Get out of here." The deputy assisted Shepherd in forcing Quinn toward the vehicle. Shepherd practically threw him in the back. His head felt like a sledgehammer had gotten the best of him. Of course, he would be dead if that were true. Right now, he wished he was.

Wait, no, he wanted to live. There was a reason to live, though at the moment, he wasn't sure what it was.

And he didn't have long to live if he didn't find a way out of this.

"You're not DEA."

"No? What makes you think that?"

"Who sent you?"

"You should have stayed in hiding. Now that you've resurfaced, you're causing all kinds of problems. But don't you worry. I'm the problem solver."

Sitting in the stuffy room where they often questioned suspects, Bree felt like a prisoner herself as she paced the small space. She would have preferred they have this heated conversation in the sheriff's office. Would the sheriff go as far as arresting her, too? Because right now, she could think of several possible charges.

How could this have happened? She rubbed her eyes.

"Bree, please calm down and hear me out," Sheriff Garrison said. "I'm your boss, and I consider myself to be a friend and a mentor to you. You're a good deputy. I know about you and Strand. You've had a thing for him—dated him in high school, too, I believe."

"What does that have to do with anything?" she asked.

The way he shrugged, it almost looked apologetic. "I thought you were getting caught up in something emotional."

Right. He probably wouldn't be having this talk with one of his male deputies. "Well, that wouldn't make me a very good deputy, now would it?"

"That's my point. You *are* a good deputy, but sometimes tragedy strikes or trauma hits. You went through a terrible experience in those woods, Bree, and then with Stevie being abducted. Sometimes we can't think with a clear mind. We make mistakes." Hurt flickered in his gaze.

Bree was ashamed that she hadn't trusted him with Stevie.

"If you'd stayed home and rested like I asked, or had even seen the counselor immediately like I requested, then maybe you wouldn't have gotten so caught up with Quinn that you let him drag you down his dark, lonely road."

His words stirred the fury inside. "His road is the road to justice, Sheriff. You would see that if you would only listen. But instead you're making things up as you go. You made it sound like I called you. Like it was all my idea."

"Well, of course. Bree, I'm trying to protect you. I needed the others to believe you were working on bringing him in. Imagine, Bree, what it looks like that you're working with a man who has a warrant for his arrest. Of course, I gave everyone the impression you were just doing your job and you had called me. As far as everyone knows, our plan was to bring Quinn in and you were holding him there for us to arrest him."

She eased into the chair. "I was holding him there to patch him up after he was *tortured* by the men who kidnapped my nephew. I had to get Stevie back. They said no cops. Quinn... He *traded* himself for Stevie. He risked his life. Does that sound like the behavior of someone leading me down some sort of dark path? He's an innocent man, Sheriff."

"I know you believe he is. I know you *want* to believe he is."

"You don't think someone who would trade his life like that, walking in there for Stevie, is a hero?"

"He might be a hero, but there's also the warrant to

consider." The sheriff scraped a hand down his face. He was running out of patience. "You're not making this easy for me to help you. You're muleheaded. Did you know that?"

Bree wasn't going to give up. She had to fight this with everything she had. "Look, Sheriff, if you think I'm a good deputy then please listen to me and believe me. A warrant out for his arrest does not mean he's guilty. There's more going on here—things you don't know—and Quinn's in a lot of danger. Keep him here in a jail cell to protect him until we can bring the true criminal to justice. Don't turn him over. Ask Agent McKesson." Bree wasn't certain she should have brought Julia into this, but she was desperate. "She knows the truth and has been helping us."

"Yes, she has been helping you. Who do you think called me to tell me where you were?"

"Wha—" The news was a punch to her gut. "No. Why would she do that?" Bree hadn't even considered it.

"She, like you, wants protection for Quinn. She said so on her call. If only *you* had trusted me enough."

"I overheard you, Sheriff. You were using me to get to him. I heard you in the hallway. 'Bree is going to bring him to us. Be aware, she doesn't know that's what she's going to do.'"

He hung his head. "I'm ashamed, Bree. Ashamed that I said those words. But at the time, I thought you were traumatized. So let's get on the same page now. I don't see any other way if we want to keep working together, do you?"

Another punch to her gut.

A nice way of threatening her with losing her job. She deserved it. "Okay. Sure. What's your plan?"

"Whatever the DEA wants with Quinn isn't my business, so much as the men who shot my deputies. I want those men. I want to know who they are and I want them incarcerated. I don't want them in my county. Tell me everything you know, Bree, and I do mean everything, so that we can get on top of this before another deputy gets shot, or someone else gets killed."

"Or abducted."

He let his head bob. "Sorry about little Stevie. But you're right. We don't want anything else like that to happen. I'm going to record our conversation, all right?"

"Okay." Bree told the sheriff everything from start to finish while she prayed nothing she said would bring more danger to Quinn. When she'd shared every detail she could think of, she released a sigh. "I hope that Julia called you because she truly felt this was the safest place for Quinn. There was so much at stake, and he's in no shape to defend himself. The reason I didn't call you at first was because I was afraid for Stevie's and Dad's lives. And because Quinn was afraid that once the wrong person, someone in law enforcement, learned he was either in the area or, in this case, behind bars, they would come for him, and he wouldn't be able to protect himself." She eyed the sheriff. "Is that going to happen, Sheriff? Please tell me you're going to protect him."

Sheriff switched off the recorder and hit the intercom. "Janet? Send a deputy to bring Quinn Strand here to see me. I'm in the interview room." Then he turned his attention back to Bree and chuckled. "You don't have to worry about that, Bree. We'll protect him as long as we can."

"That won't be long. You're going to have to turn him over to those who issued the warrant."

"Not if I have charges of my own, which I'm working on. That process could take a while. Give us some time to figure this out."

"Do you believe me then?" she asked.

"I think you believe it. I'm holding out for the evidence that proves something decisive either way. He saved Stevie and he protected you, and that goes a long way. It tells me something, so I want to give him the benefit of a doubt."

Bobby opened the door without knocking. "Sheriff?"

The sheriff frowned. "Where's Strand? I asked for someone to bring me Strand."

"He isn't here."

"What are you talking about?"

"They took him."

The sheriff stood. "They? Who's they?"

The deputy paled. "DEA. Had the paperwork authorizing the transfer."

SIXTEEN

In a daze, Bree exited the sheriff's department and headed to her vehicle in the parking lot.

Snap out of it. Quinn needs you. She couldn't let herself dwell on the way that her department had failed so magnificently. The knowledge could break her if she wasn't careful. She sucked in a breath and hurried the last few feet to her county vehicle. She wasn't in her uniform, but time was of the essence.

They looked at the security footage of the bouncer-looking guy leaving with Quinn. Special Forces, if she had to guess. Quinn could usually hold his own, except he wasn't in the best condition right now. Physically or emotionally, if he really thought Bree had made that phone call.

She was still stunned to learn that Julia—the agent he had trusted—had made that call.

The paperwork had been correct, but the sheriff contacted Stan Rollins, the man Quinn had mentioned, and learned it wasn't an authorized pickup, after all. All the information had been forged in their system and in person. They weren't able to identify this man.

Or if the DEA did know who the mystery man was, they were keeping it to themselves.

So now Bree and other deputies were looking for Quinn. She hoped she wasn't too late. Other vehicles left the parking lot in search of their abducted inmate and the man who took him right out from under their noses.

She'd never seen the sheriff so incensed, even after what she'd put him through.

She forced back the tears. Now wasn't the time to get emotional. She really had to work on pushing that side of her away.

With the key fob, she unlocked the vehicle and glanced up. Across the street she spotted a familiar woman learning against her car.

Julia. Bree rushed across the parking lot, crossed the street and got in her face, wanting to rail at her.

In fact, she wanted to punch her.

Julia frowned. "Go ahead and hit me if it will make you feel any better, but I'd rather spend my time trying to help Quinn."

"Why did you call my sheriff? What were you thinking?"

"It was the only way to protect him."

"Protect him? He could be dead now. Some guy claiming to be a DEA agent took him."

"What?"

The incredulity in her voice said it all. Julia really didn't know.

"He said his name was Shepherd. I'm going to look for him now. That's why deputies are all speeding out of the lot, or didn't you notice?"

"Bree, have you forgotten…"

She sucked in air. "Oh! He has a tracker in him."

"Do you think it still works?" Julia asked.

"Yes. Let's take my car!" Bree jogged with Julia over to her department vehicle and they got in.

"Hurry up, let's get moving," Julia said.

Bree peeled out of the parking space. "I can hurry up and turn right or hurry up and turn left. Where is he?"

"Just a second, I'm still pulling up the software." A moment later, Julia said, "Take a right, I think."

Bree swerved out of the parking lot.

God, please help us find him.

"Okay, keep talking. Where is he in general, and then you can give me the details? I should call the other deputies out there. They might be able to find him." She lifted the radio from the dash.

Julia pressed her hand over Bree's. "Think, Bree. Those deputies will only lock him up again, which is obviously more dangerous than we knew. This isn't going to stop. We have to find another way to help him."

Bree replaced the radio. *I sure hope you understand this time, Sheriff Garrison.*

Julia stared at her tablet. "Shepherd has a good head start and is already driving out of town. Take the next exit."

Speeding down a two-lane state highway, Bree took the exit. At first, she had the lights flashing. But then she turned them off. Better not to alert the others if she was going to go down this road with Quinn again.

"Where is he now?"

Julia looked at her screen, but hesitated. "The fact that he's still moving is a good sign."

"What do you mean? What aren't you saying?"

"It means that Shepherd hasn't killed him and dumped his body somewhere."

Nausea rushed through her. "That's not all that comforting. He could have killed him already and is looking for the right place to dump him." Bree couldn't believe she said the words out loud.

"I was trying to remain positive."

A lump formed in Bree's throat. "Right. Good idea."

Weaving in and out of traffic, Bree pressed the accelerator, nearly flooring it. "What do you know about this Shepherd guy?"

"Nothing. He could be impersonating an agent." Julia looked at her tablet again. "Take another right. Just up here." She pointed to a road on the right.

"Uh-oh."

Bree didn't like the sound of that. "What is it?"

"It's the dot. It's slowing down."

Her pulse jumped. "Maybe that means we can catch up to him."

"I hope you're right."

What Julia wasn't saying was that they could be too late.

Bree's heart hammered. "Just so you know, Julia, I considered calling the sheriff, too, like you. But I didn't call him because… I thought we would decide that together. I thought we were working together as a team."

Julia blew out an exasperated breath. "Don't you see? Quinn would never have agreed to that. And I'm sorry you don't feel you can trust me completely, but you must trust me to a point or you wouldn't be with me now."

Bree slowed the vehicle enough to turn onto the bumpy dirt road Julia indicated. Unfortunately, she knew where it led. To the spot where the river met the bay.

A shudder crawled over her. *Quinn…oh Lord, please save him!* "I don't like this."

Julia chambered a round in her Glock 22. The same model that Bree carried. "We'd better be prepared," Julia said. "I have a feeling this guy plays for keeps.

We can't show him any sign of weakness if we're going to take Quinn alive."

Please, let us not be too late.

Julia pressed her hand to Bree's arm as she stared at the tablet. "We should get out now. We need to walk. Approach slowly."

"I don't know. Maybe I need to speed through here and mow the guy down before he kills Quinn." Could she trust Julia? Was she making a mistake?

Despite her words, she followed Julia's instructions. She steered the vehicle off the road. It rocked over the potholes until she stopped next to a particularly thick group of trees, whose foliage scraped against the car. She glanced at Julia. "For good measure. Just to hide our presence."

Julia nodded. "We don't need any more men hunting you or Quinn."

"Or you, now that you've chosen to accept this mission."

The woman gave a half smile at Bree's reference to *Mission: Impossible.*

Before Bree climbed from the vehicle, she reached to radio-dispatch her status, then remembered they couldn't risk the other deputies joining them and Quinn getting jailed again. She grabbed her own weapon. She got out and quietly shut the door. She followed Julia through the woods, this scenario bringing memories rushing back. Images of her time on the run with Quinn through the green temperate rain forest at night, and then the day when he got her as far as the edge of town.

She shook off the memories.

Would this ever end? Would her life ever go back to normal or be the same again?

Julia suddenly backed against a tree.

Bree did the same. She was at the woman's mercy at the moment—only Julia had the tablet allowing her to follow the tracking device inside Quinn. Bree needed to prepare herself for the possibility that Julia was lying and this was a trap. She didn't want to believe that, but at this moment, she was wary of just about everyone.

Still, Quinn had trusted her enough to bring her into this, so Bree would do her best to have confidence in Julia while remaining cautious.

The sounds of nature surrounded her. Crickets and frogs. Birds. What was Julia waiting on? She just kept staring at the tablet.

"Julia," Bree whispered.

The woman pressed a finger to her lips and looked at her like she was an idiot.

Bree peered around the tree. Did Julia see someone? Is that why she asked her to keep quiet? Bree didn't see anyone. She was done waiting. She made her way quietly forward in the same direction they'd been tracking.

Julia caught up with her and grabbed her arm. "What are you doing?"

"I'm searching for Quinn."

The woman frowned and shook her head. "I lost the signal."

"What do you mean you lost it?"

She shoved the tablet at Bree. "Look. It's gone. Just... nothing."

Quinn stared at the gash in his arm where Shepherd had cut the tracker out. The man must have known about Quinn's experience being shuffled from one warehouse to another and had figured out how Quinn had been found. Either that or he'd seen someone following them.

Maybe that was why Shepherd had taken the detour down the road to the bay. He'd parked and yanked Quinn out. Searched Quinn's clothing, and then ensued a painful search along his arms, the most likely place the tracker would be inserted. He'd pinpointed a couple of places that were false positives, as it were, slicing into Quinn at will until he found the small chip.

He held it between his fingers, then crushed it in his palm. "These things could cause cancer, you know."

Really. Quinn held back his retort to that insane statement.

"I should have figured something like this." The oversize ex-marine kept shaking his head.

Blood rushed down Quinn's arm and onto the wet sand of the small pebbled beach where the river hit the bay. Water lapped up and washed the blood away, and the evidence.

What now?

Why didn't Shepherd just kill Quinn here and dump his body and get it over with? Quinn didn't want to ask him that or give him any ideas. "You're taking me to someone." His guess would be Declan.

Had to be it. Quinn had a price on his head and apparently everyone—the good and the bad—were after him. Except he suspected this man Shepherd had been hired by Declan, who wanted Quinn dead before he could tell Michael Jones that Declan was DEA undercover, and Declan had been the one to steal the money. Declan had also conveniently leaked to the DEA that Quinn was a dirty agent and had stolen the money.

"You're smarter than I figured."

What was that supposed to mean? Quinn huffed, which brought on pain. He wouldn't talk to this guy more than necessary. Needed to save his energy for the big moment.

Coming up soon.

Knowing that kept him waiting.

The guy was always sarcastic in his tone, insulting and intimidating. Maybe that's because he didn't have the moves to back up his attitude. He wrapped Quinn's arm so blood wouldn't get in his vehicle. If he was trying to avoid DNA evidence, he'd have to try harder—especially with Quinn awake and determined to leave as much behind as he could, including some blood. Just in case the big moment didn't materialize like he imagined and he ended up dead somewhere. His DNA in this vehicle, should investigators look that closely, would give them answers.

"Now. Get in." Shepherd looked at him with those crazy eyes.

Quinn had no intention of getting back in—not willingly, anyway. The big moment was now.

"No." He head-butted Shepherd and in one smooth motion moved behind him and wrapped his cuffed wrists around his throat. "Now. Drop your gun."

Shepherd said nothing. His face turned red. Veins popped out at his temples. He squirmed and fought. He mumbled something that sounded like, "I'm going to kill you."

"Oh yeah?" Quinn pulled even tighter. "I don't think so. Now. Drop the gun so I don't have to kill *you*."

Shepherd opened his hand and released the gun. It clattered on the pebbles. Quinn kept the pressure steady. He had no intention of releasing Shepherd until he was unconscious. Alive, but down for the count. Finally, Shepherd went limp. Quinn eased him to the ground and checked his pulse. Look at that—he had a heart, after all.

He pocketed the gun, grateful he hadn't been made to change into the usual jail jumpsuit. Then he searched Shepherd. Found another gun and two knives.

Bingo. Keys to the cuffs.

Quinn freed himself. He hurried to search the vehicle. *Aha.* Duct tape. Shepherd might have planned to use this on Quinn, but those tables had been turned. He pulled a long strip out, tore it with his teeth, then wrapped Shepherd's wrists.

"Much more elegant than handcuffs, don't you think?"

Shepherd remained unconscious. Good. Quinn dragged him over to a tree and leaned him up against it. He taped his ankles together, too. He'd let Bree and Julia know where to find him. They could communicate with Sheriff Garrison that they had found a problem that needed solving.

Time for Quinn to go his own way and end this himself. He'd face off with Declan and get him to confess. That was the only option left to him. He couldn't let himself be caged again only to be removed for disposal.

The "problem solver" stirred. "You're a dead man."

"Not by your hands. I'm thinking you're in bigger trouble than I am." Declan would dispose of Shepherd to eliminate the risk of Shepherd flipping on him in a plea deal.

"They'll kill you when they find you," the man muttered.

"They have to find me first."

"You shouldn't have dragged the other agent into this. Both women are going to die now. The plans are already in motion."

Quinn sucked in a breath. "When and where?"

The man spit at him.

Tugging the cell from Shepherd's pocket, he scrolled through the numbers. "I'm going to call Declan and tell him what I've done to you and where to come and get you if you don't tell me right now what you know so that I can protect them. And if you're not telling me the truth, I'll tell Michael Jones, and his hit man, too."

Genuine fear shone in Shepherd's eyes. "Okay, okay. I'll tell you, but you won't make it in time."

SEVENTEEN

Bree steered into her driveway and waved at her neighbor, who got into her car. Bree had made sure it was returned earlier in the day. Julia pulled to the curb in her own vehicle. Bree sat in her car for a minute and hung her head. Rubbed her neck. What did she do now?

They'd come across the man who'd taken Quinn from the cell, but he wasn't talking. His hands and feet were bound and he wasn't going anywhere. She assumed Quinn had escaped.

Before they'd found Shepherd, they'd heard a vehicle exiting down the road from the bay. She surmised that must have been Quinn escaping in Shepherd's vehicle.

Why didn't he call her? Contact her?

Maybe he wanted to do this on his own—he probably thought she'd call the sheriff and she was the reason he'd been sent to jail.

One thing for certain—she now knew that he'd been right all along. He was in danger sitting in a jail cell.

Julia knocked on the car door window, startling Bree.

Reluctantly, she climbed out. She wished she could escape Julia just for a few minutes. She needed to decompress. But there was no time and they needed to work together on Quinn's behalf. At least she had Julia working with her and she finally had the sheriff behind her. Since his department had let him be taken by a fake agent, the sheriff was furious, and more apt to believe Quinn's story. To believe Bree. He had his hands full with interrogating Shepherd at the moment.

Though she walked slowly, she realized she wasn't limping anymore. A small victory. Bree paused to scan the yard and the street.

"If you insist on coming to your house, can we just go inside already?" Julia sounded spooked.

Bree unlocked her door and welcomed the familiar space. But her home, usually filled with laughter and love, was empty. It felt cold and dead without Stevie and Dad.

"What are we doing, Julia? Quinn probably won't reach out to either of us. And if he doesn't, I have no idea what to do next to help him. But you do. You must know who is behind this. The guy he mentioned—Declan."

"Yes. I know him. Unfortunately, I don't have any evidence that he's done anything wrong, whereas Quinn still has a warrant out for his arrest. All I can do is go back to my division headquarters in New Orleans and try to convince my superior about what is going on. He was also Quinn's superior, so he might be willing to listen."

"But your life is in danger now, too, Julia, isn't it?"

She nodded. "It's a dangerous career to begin with, not unlike your own."

Bree shook her head. "Here in this county, we don't come across this kind of criminal activity that often. Or at all, I should say. Until a few days ago, I had never had a need to pull my weapon on anyone, much less shoot them." She shuddered. "I thought my job would consist of warning people to uphold the law, especially on waterways, since I've been working the marine division. But never anything like this. You, however—it's part of your job to investigate and arrest the worst sorts of criminals, at least that's what Quinn told me. Cartels and drug dealers."

"Sit down and rest. I'll get you some water or something from the kitchen," Julia said.

"No. This is my house. You sit down. I'll get us something to drink. Maybe I'll even cook some dinner to clear my mind." Her heart ached. This was all wrong.

She glanced at Julia, who took a seat on the sofa. Bree didn't know how Julia could live with herself after calling the sheriff to report Quinn's whereabouts, especially after what happened.

"So what do you think he'll do next?" she spoke loudly so Julia could hear her out in the living area.

Julia approached and leaned on the counter. "I don't know. He might go back into hiding. Or he might face Declan or even Michael Jones. That's what I believe he'll do because otherwise, he always has to worry about your safety. The Quinn I know will face this head-on this time."

Bree set a couple of soft drinks and a bag of chips and some salsa on the counter. "I hope you like tacos. I'm thawing the meat in the microwave right now."

A racket by the door drew their attention. Bree grabbed her gun. She wasn't even safe in her own home.

Quinn stumbled inside. Bree stared at him, taking in the sight of him, unable to comprehend that he was here.

"Quinn! You're all right."

"We have to get out!" His tone was urgent. It scared her.

"Wait. What?"

"Now!"

She reached for her bag on the coffee table. Tried to set the plates down. He grabbed Bree, who then dropped the food, and dragged her out the door, running. Julia was close behind.

"Faster! We have to run!"

He pushed Bree until she thought she would fall on her face.

An explosion resounded, the shock wave pushing them to the ground.

Quinn covered Bree and Julia both, protecting them with his larger bulk. Protecting them because that's what he did. He gasped for breath. Endured the pain of the blast. Pain upon more pain until he almost felt numb from it all.

He almost hadn't made it in time—Shepherd's vehicle got a flat tire, of all things! And Shepherd's cell was dead. He had no way to communicate with Bree. He'd cut across neighborhood yards, sprinting as fast as he could, hoping and praying she wouldn't come home before he got to her to warn her.

At least they had made it across the street. He'd taken a dive behind two parked cars when the blast went off.

God, please let no one else be hurt.

"Is it over?" Bree asked.

Julia scrambled to her feet. Quinn remained on the ground, but he rolled so Bree wouldn't be pinned. "Are you okay?" he asked.

Gratitude filled her gaze. "I am now."

Quinn watched flames engulf what was left of the house that Bree had shared with Stevie and her father.

He tried to remain unmoved by Bree's tears. Her shoulders shaking. She'd been through more than anyone should ever have to go through. This was just another example of his life destroying hers.

Julia crouched next to them. "How did you know, Quinn?"

"Shepherd told me."

"And you believed him?"

Quinn tugged a cell from his pocket. "I threatened to call Declan and tell them how he'd messed up—and where to find him."

Finally, he pushed to his feet. When this was over he would sleep for a month—but hopefully that wouldn't be in a jail cell. Since he didn't know for sure where he'd end up, that meant he couldn't sleep until he'd done everything he could to ensure justice was served and he was absolved while he still had the freedom to act.

Bree grabbed his arm and turned him to face her. "I was so worried about you."

He wanted to pull her into his arms. He'd almost forgotten her betrayal, and he wouldn't so easily let himself trust her. Still, he'd make sure she was safe. He'd protect her by resolving this on his own.

He started to walk away. She grabbed him again. He winced and she let go.

"Quinn, you have to know that I didn't call the sheriff."

"Right." He knew she was saying this to make him feel better. "You thought you were protecting me. I get it."

"She didn't call him," Julia said. "I did."

"You?" His brain had already been shaken, but that news stunned him. He took a step back.

"We both wanted to protect you," Julia said. "We both thought you'd be safer in custody. The difference is that Bree would have asked your permission, and I knew you would never give it. So I made the call without consulting you, Quinn."

"Well, you see what a mistake that was."

"Yes. I see now. I'm sorry. So now what?" Julia had an innate ability to remain unemotional and calculating—the complete opposite of Bree in almost every way.

"We get out of here, for starters," he said.

"Looks like your car is toast," Julia said to Bree.

Part of the roof had landed on Bree's county vehicle.

"We'll have to take mine," Julia said. "Come on. People are starting to gather. It doesn't look like anyone was hurt. No other houses were affected. But one of the men after you might be here to make sure we died in the explosion."

"If so, he would have seen us leave the house before it exploded."

"Maybe not." Julia led them to her rental car and pulled her keys from her pocket to unlock the vehicle. They got in and she drove away from the obliterated home. "Call your sheriff to tell him you weren't in the house, but that you're a target now and you'll contact him as soon as you can. After all of this, he won't pretend he can protect you, Bree."

Bree agreed and made the call, then directed her words to Quinn.

"Quinn…" She hesitated. The way she said his name, he wished he could just curl up with her and forget any of this was happening. Pretend that they had no tragic past.

"You might find this hard to believe," she continued, "but Sheriff Garrison is sorry about what happened. He was ready to talk to you about what he could do to help you. He wanted to give you a chance. That's when we found out they had already come to take you. Quinn, he wants to protect you."

"He can't even protect you, Bree. That's why you're not going anywhere someone can find you."

"Even so, he wants to help us. So let's use him as a resource if we have to."

How did he make her understand? "He can't help me with what comes next, and besides, there is no 'us' anymore."

The words came out wrong, or maybe he heard them wrong—his own words.

"What do you mean?"

"Julia is going to take you somewhere safe and protect you while I end this."

"Please, can you at least tell us what you're planning?"

"Yes. And I'm going to need Julia's help."

He had a feeling he was hurting Bree by leaving her out, but he was only protecting her.

"I'm on board for anything you need from me," Julia said. "But first, where are we going? Once they decide they need to find you, Bree, and maybe even you, Quinn, it won't take them long to figure out they're looking for my vehicle."

"I have a safe house. I stayed at a motel, not wanting to use the safe house yet. I hoped I wouldn't have to. It's hard to believe that things have gotten that much worse. But I think we're at that point." He directed Julia to the place—a last resort, really. He was glad he had made those arrangements.

A forty-five-minute drive later, they settled into a cabin in the woods on the far side of Coldwater Bay. It belonged to his friend who also owned the deer lease where he'd been hiding. Quinn cleaned up, aware both women were waiting to hear his plans. He wasn't exactly sure how much he wanted to share, except he did need Julia's help. Even though she'd called the sheriff on him, she'd come through so far so he believed he could trust her.

He exited the restroom, having donned his friend's clothes from the closet. They smelled stale like the cabin, but better than carrying the odor of jail cell and river rot.

Bree and Julia were whispering when he entered the living area. "Now I feel like a million dollars."

Julia flashed a smile, that familiar look in her eyes, before she angled a knowing look at Bree. He thought at one time that Julia was interested in him, but she knew he could never care about anyone like he had once cared about Bree.

Now to convince Bree of his plan. He walked toward her and crouched in front of her.

Took her hand in his. He might not ever see her again. He wasn't sure his heart could take that. He once thought he couldn't love, because then he'd be left alone.

The alternative was just as bad.

Maybe it was worth the risk.

"You're scaring me, Quinn. What...what are you going to say?" She watched him.

He smiled with a huff, then moved to sit next to her.

"Should I give you two some privacy to talk?" Julia asked with a grin.

"No. We all need to talk about what comes next," he said.

"Please do share your elaborate plans with us. We've been waiting long enough."

"I hadn't exactly figured it out then, but now that we're all here together and hopefully safe for the time being, I think I've got it."

He tugged Shepherd's cell out again. "All the key players are on this cell. The numbers."

"You could use that as evidence," Julia said. "Case closed."

"And have it disappear in the evidence room? Been there. Done that. I can't hang my life on this one thing."

"Then what?" Bree asked.

"I'm going to call my nemesis. Agent Declan Miller."

"He'll be expecting you to pull something." Julia rose from the chair and put her hands on her slender hips.

"I'll tell him I want to meet him face-to-face," Quinn said, "and that I have evidence against him."

Julia threw her hands in the air. "Oh, is that all. He'll scoff and say if you had evidence you wouldn't be calling him. He'd be getting arrested. You know it's true. I know it's true."

"He'll believe I really have evidence if I convince him I'm going to negotiate with him for a piece of the pie rather than turning him in."

"You're…"

"Working undercover. Isn't that what we do? Only this time, it's on my own behalf. I can get a confession from him then. He'll have to admit he stole the money in the first place. I'll say I just want everyone off my back, or else I'm going to tell Michael he's behind stealing the money. So that's my deal to him. That's my offer. If he doesn't take it, he risks being in as much trouble as I am, and since he actually did steal it, they'll kill him. He fears them more than he fears the DEA."

"I don't know, Quinn." Bree looked at him. She took his hand and squeezed. "That sounds too risky."

"And what is it you want me to do?" Julia asked.

"You're going to arrange for Stan to be there, nearby, watching and listening to the whole thing."

She rolled her head back and laughed. "Just how am I supposed to do that?"

"Oh, come on, Julia. Everyone knows you get what you want. I know you'll think of something."

"You're sure you wouldn't just rather go into hiding?" she asked. "This is a huge risk. Joke about it if you want, but I can't promise I can deliver."

He glanced down at Bree sitting next to him. "Sometimes you have to take a risk if you want to live free and whole."

Bree must have sensed the other meaning behind his words. She angled her head to look in his eyes. She'd lost the hurt and anguish, the disappointment in him he'd once seen. Now he saw something of fear for him and hope. Could there be hope for them? A future for them?

He'd have to hold on to that hope through this, since he no longer had that picture of her.

EIGHTEEN

As he stared down at her, Bree could almost imagine them alone together and nothing else going on around them. There were no bad guys or good guys after either of them to tear them apart once and for all.

He cared for her. She saw that in his eyes, knew it to be true, but the guy was always a runner when it came to commitment. Would he run again this time, when this was finally over?

For the first time in her life, though she'd been hurt so many times by him, she thought she might not care so much about the risks. She wasn't afraid. She just wanted time with him no matter how short that time was. How crazy was that?

Thinking that way was beyond ridiculous. On the other hand, how many times had Dad set her up with someone else? Or encouraged her to marry so that Stevie could have a father figure once Dad was gone? He wouldn't live forever, he'd said.

She'd dated others, but no one had come close to making her feel this way.

Had her heart always been holding out for Quinn— an impossible dream, at that?

But at this moment, it didn't seem all that impossible. "I don't want you to go. I don't want you to do this."

He turned her to face him completely. "I know. I don't want to do it, but it's not that much more dangerous than what I did before when working undercover."

"Julia and I will come with you and help you," Bree said. She didn't think she would convince him but she had to try.

"No. You're not going with me, Bree. I can't possibly concentrate on what I need to do knowing you could be in danger."

"He's right, Bree," Julia said. "You'd be a distraction for him. He's good at what he does. Or at least, he was until he started getting much too close to the truth—that Declan was stealing from Michael Jones. Once Declan suspected Quinn was onto him, he set Quinn up—so both the DEA and Michael are after him."

"Except you, Julia. You're not after him. Why not? Why help him?" Bree asked.

Julia frowned. "At first, it was about saving Stevie. Now, I have to see this through. Besides, I've known Quinn and worked with him for long enough. I trust him."

Okay.

Quinn cleared his throat. "So you're going to stay here with Bree to make sure she doesn't go anywhere. Make sure she listens to reason, and then you're going to figure out how to get Stan to our meeting place— my job is to get a confession. It's the only way. Can you handle that? Do you have a plan yet?"

"Sure. I'm going to tell him the truth. It's going to take him several hours to get here. We both have our work cut out for us. It could take Stan hours if he even agrees."

"I'll be waiting," Quinn said. There was also the chance that Declan would not take the bait.

Bree shoved herself up from the sofa. Rubbing her arms, she stared out the window into the woods. "And what am I supposed to do? Nothing? Sit here and wait?" For the bad news that Quinn had been killed?

He stood and caught her against him. Hugged her as if it would be the last time. "So I can know you're safe, Bree. For me, okay? They can use you to get to me. You know that."

She didn't answer him.

An hour later, he drove off in Julia's car and she watched him through the window. "How long do we have to wait here?"

"As long as it takes." Julia paced with her weapon out as if she thought someone would come bursting through the door any minute.

"I can protect myself, you know."

"Yep. You're good at what you do, but so am I." Julia stopped pacing and stared at Bree. "There's something I don't get."

"Join the club." Bree grabbed a bottled water—compliments of Quinn, who had the foresight to set this safe house up. She plopped on the sofa. This could be a very long wait.

"No, I mean about you two."

"Like I said, join the club."

"Seriously. You guys obviously have feelings for each other. He mentioned you dated before. So why aren't you already married with a bunch of kids?"

"Now that's a long story."

"We have all night."

"I was kind of hoping it wouldn't take that long." Bree took a swig and then she told Julia everything. Girl talk. She really liked the woman, and could see herself doing this on a stakeout with Julia. "Now it's your turn to spill. You know all about my messy feelings, so dish on whoever your crush might be."

"Well, there is this guy. I could really get into him. Could love him. I think he could love me, too. I know he's attracted to me, but he's not good with commitment."

"I so get that."

"I know you do. In my case, though, there's always this other woman he thinks about. He really can't be free to love until she's gone." Julia looked at her long and hard.

Oh. "You… Are you talking about Quinn and me? You're in love with Quinn." It wasn't a question. Her heart seized up at the realization that her life was in danger for a different reason.

Her gun was two feet away from her.

Julia still held hers.

"Oh, please. I'm not going to shoot you."

Bree had obviously telegraphed her thoughts. She wasn't trained in working undercover like Julia and Quinn. "Then what?"

"I could never find a way to make it work until now. Like Quinn said, I know how to negotiate for what I want."

Sweat trickled down his brow at the old warehouse along the river that emptied into Coldwater Bay. The same warehouse where he'd traded himself for Stevie. The perfect place to meet with Declan. Dark and abandoned. What better place to face off with a dirty DEA agent?

He waited in the rafters so he could see who was coming and going before he made his presence known.

Still, his view was more limited than he would have liked.

In this situation, he couldn't wear a wire. He didn't have the equipment, and there would be no one listening on the other end. He couldn't record the conversation. That could work against him as well. Declan would be expecting that. This man knew all Quinn's tricks. They had worked for the same agency. Besides, there hadn't been time. He would work this as long as necessary to get the evidence he needed. But if Julia did her part and had success, this could all be over today.

I hope you came through for me, Julia.

He was counting on her. Their superior would be more likely to listen to her—a good, upstanding agent without a warrant out for her arrest. As Quinn thought back to the chain of events that had brought him here, he knew that all paths led to this one place.

He would have had to get a confession out of Declan to end it once and for all. Nothing else would be evidence enough for Declan's uncle, who happened to be Stan's boss.

All he could do was count on Julia to put her piece into place—Stan Rollins. Then he could hear the truth for himself, once and for all. Quinn knew that his boss wanted to believe in him, but Quinn had to give him the evidence he needed. Declan had everyone chasing after Quinn. This was a case of two DEA agents accusing each other, one of whom had an important connection within the organization. And that wasn't Quinn.

When his cover had been blown, Quinn had left, at Stan's urging, and when Michael Jones discovered missing money, Quinn had become an easy scapegoat for Declan.

He knew it was only a matter of time before the truth

came out about Declan. He was just speeding up the inevitable. All the pieces were in place. His plan to trap the man would work. It had to. Quinn exhaled louder than he'd wanted.

An aluminum can clanked across the broken concrete. Then he spotted a silhouette in the doorway—light from the outside shining into the darkened warehouse turned the man into a shadow. But Quinn recognized that frame and stance.

"Strand. I'm here. Just like you asked. Now show yourself."

Quinn had a plan, but he knew Declan wouldn't show up here without one of his own. What was it? He had to hope that he was adequately prepared for anything.

Carefully he climbed down until he could drop to the floor. He landed on his feet.

"Did you bring the evidence?" Declan asked.

"Maybe."

"I don't have time to play games," he said. "I could arrest you right here and now."

"You could." But Quinn knew he wouldn't. Declan didn't want Quinn telling anyone what he knew—that's why he had sent Shepherd to kill him.

"Tell me what you want." Declan remained in the doorway.

The plan came down to this one moment. Quinn drew on his years of undercover work. He had to be convincing. "I want a percentage of the money you stole."

"What are you talking about? I didn't steal anything. You did."

"Come on, man. We both know you stole it and accused me. If you didn't, then why are you here to get the evidence I have on you? Now who's playing games?"

Declan's shadowed face remained dark. Quinn wished

he could see the sweat beading on his temples. "Listen, just tell me what you want."

"I already told you." Quinn took a step closer. "I want in on the embezzling. Why didn't you come to me in the first place instead of blowing my cover? We could have worked something out then."

"Get real. I couldn't trust you. And I don't trust you now."

"I'm not asking you to trust me. Just cut me in on your enterprise to steal from Michael Jones. We can put the blame on someone else for the stolen money."

He laughed. "You mean like Julia?"

No. He hadn't meant that. But Julia and Stan should be here already, somewhere close and listening.

God, please let it be so.

Quinn shrugged noncommittally, letting Declan interpret that as he saw fit.

"All right. I'll cut you in on the money. But it might not be so easy to clear things up with Michael."

"You can make that happen. You're not getting the evidence until Michael removes the price on my head." Quinn stared down Declan. "Make him believe I'm just a dirty DEA agent working undercover. I know you'll do what you must to get the evidence I have against you."

"Yes, I'll do what I have to." He thrust his hand to the side behind the wall where Quinn couldn't see.

Quinn tugged his weapon out, expecting a gunfight, and aimed it at Declan.

He yanked Bree over next to him. He pressed his weapon against her head and laughed. "I'm disappointed in you, Strand. You're not the agent I thought you were. Now toss the evidence along with your gun or I'm going to shoot her in the head. Oh, and I'll be shooting her with your weapon. Wait. No, this is Bree's weapon. You shot a deputy with her gun. See how easy it is to make it look like this is all on you?"

Unfortunately, he did. What had happened to Julia? How had Declan found Bree? He tossed the gun over.

"Now I want the cell phone you used to call me. I know you took it off Shepherd. I also know that's the evidence you hoped to use against me."

"I don't know what you're talking about."

"I know all about what you've been up to. You thought you were so smart hiding in the mountains near Coldwater Bay, but I had someone follow you. Didn't want you turning things around on me. Then when you ended up in jail, I knew it was time for Shepherd to end things before you convinced Michael I had stolen the money. Now that will never happen. Give me the phone."

Declan jabbed his weapon against her temple and Bree winced, but she didn't cry out. Quinn couldn't let her presence shift his focus or she would die today.

"I know all about your plan," Declan continued with a sneer.

Wait. Julia? Had she given him up? If Julia had given him up, then Stan wasn't anywhere close to listen to their conversation. At the moment, Quinn couldn't care about exonerating himself—he was more concerned with the idea that there was no backup, no one coming to help them. Bree was once again in a life-threatening situation because of him.

He could never catch a break.

Though he wouldn't believe Julia would do that, what did it matter now if he couldn't save Bree?

"I'm not tossing the phone until I have Bree next to me."

Declan fired his weapon into the ground, then aimed

it at her gut. "I can keep shooting so you can watch her suffer. The next one goes into her abdomen so she can bleed out and die in front of you. Then I'll shoot you and take what I want from your body."

Quinn believed him. He tossed the cell over.

NINETEEN

Declan's tight grip would leave a bruise, but that was the least of her worries. He forced her into the boat. She stumbled forward. She had to do something to escape, but what? When she peered around at him, he pointed the weapon at her. "Don't think I won't shoot you if you make trouble for me. I'll make you suffer before you die. Understand?"

"Yes." But she would find a way to turn this around, one way or another.

"Move or I'll start shooting."

"I got it."

He turned his back to her and started the boat. Steered it upriver. She knew he would be meeting up with someone who would take him out of Coldwater Bay. She'd heard him on his cell. Declan would escape, leaving no evidence that he'd ever been there at all. Everything he'd done would be pinned on his chosen target as he once again claimed Quinn was the bad guy.

The villain. The person who had murdered Bree. She had no doubt that's what Declan intended for her, but for now he used her for leverage.

That, however, had not been part of Julia's negotiation with him. Oh, Julia wanted Bree dead, all right—

but Julia needed Quinn to be exonerated so they could be together. Declan must have agreed to clear Quinn's name, but he'd gone back on his word. Julia had believed she could outsmart Declan, but couldn't she see that guy was never going to go through with his agreement? Bree had tried to tell her. To plead with her. To warn her.

When Declan had come to the cabin to take Bree, he'd then shot Julia.

Bree could crumble under the weight of it all, but she had to be strong. Once again for Stevie.

For Dad.

And this time…for Quinn. He needed her to survive. He needed her help.

She was the only person who had heard the confession and could be the witness to Declan's admission of his crimes.

Oh, Lord, please help us.

All she knew was that she had to get the upper hand before Declan got to his destination. If she jumped from the boat, he would just steer it around and shoot her in the water. Too risky. She'd been in that position before and had barely survived.

She had to bide her time for the right moment.

Her hair whipped around her face and eyes as the boat continued to speed. Behind her, she spotted another boat gaining on them.

Quinn!

She hoped Declan hadn't spotted him yet. He'd shot at Quinn, who'd taken a dive out of the line of fire and hidden in the warehouse. Bree feared Declan would keep shooting until he knew Quinn was dead, but Quinn had fired back with a weapon he'd hidden away. Declan had apparently decided that a shoot-out would take too long. He had other plans and didn't have time to waste. He'd used Bree as a human shield as he rushed her to the waiting boat.

She didn't know where he had gotten a boat, but that was definitely Quinn behind them, even though Declan had threatened to kill her if Quinn followed. Others were on the river fishing, so maybe Quinn thought he would just blend in and Declan wouldn't notice.

But Bree wasn't going to wait for him to save the day. She knew how to protect herself and get out of this. She'd find her moment soon, and then she'd reunite with Quinn. Had he figured out Julia's double cross? Bree hadn't expected the role Julia would play. By her own admission, Julia hadn't planned on it or even known how to get rid of Bree, then the opportunity had presented itself. Or so Julia thought.

That plan had backfired on her big-time. Bree hoped that Julia had survived the bullet. She had her own cell and could call 911. Bree couldn't help her now.

Bree shifted her focus to saving herself and Quinn. She watched the man at the helm.

At this point, Declan likely believed she was someone he could intimidate and scare, and he paid no attention to her in the back. Had he forgotten her? She crept forward. Then he swerved hard to the right, and she fell against the seat. Then hard to the left.

Then he accelerated. Going this fast up a river, slamming over rapids and boulders, was dangerous. But he was determined to keep her pinned in her seat. She looked behind them. Quinn was catching up. He had a faster boat.

Declan glanced over his shoulder. He fired his weapon, maybe hoping a random shot would accidentally hit Quinn. Or her. She wasn't sure which, but when he focused on steering and powering the boat up over a patch of rapids and around a group of boulders, she crept forward again.

He twisted his arm behind him to fire the weapon. Now!

She grabbed that arm and twisted it further up his back, driving it high into his shoulder blades, the weapon firing off several times before he dropped it. He shoved the throttle forward and the boat picked up more speed. She almost lost her footing, but in the interim, he turned on her.

He couldn't see what she saw.

Dead ahead, the boat headed straight toward a boulder in the river. She pointed and shouted, "You're going to kill us!"

He didn't seem to hear her or care what she'd said. Ignoring her warning, he reached for her throat. The boat hit the rock and skidded across the top, arced into the air and twisted, then capsized, dumping them in the river. She brushed up against boulders. Pain sliced through her shoulder. Bree held her breath and tried to force her way up to breach the surface in the strong current. The boat started sinking, the motor still running. Eventually it would flood and stop, but until then, the blades could shred her. She thrashed to escape it, the river finally pulling her and the boat apart.

Bree swam toward the surface again. She broke through and sucked in air, working to keep her head above the water. She allowed the river to carry her until she could swim toward the riverbank.

Where was Quinn? How far back was he? Had Declan survived?

As she swam, she looked over her shoulder. Tried to

remain aware of her surroundings. She didn't want to be in the water with Declan if he came for her again.

Something gripped her leg and yanked.

Looking down, she saw that Declan had a hold of her.

"No! Leave me alone!" She fought and thrashed.

He pulled her toward him, then pushed her face in the water.

He wanted to drown her. She fought his grip as her lungs screamed. She hadn't had the chance to suck in enough air. She tried to find a rock to hit him with. Her fingers dug into the earth around one but she couldn't get it. It was in too deep.

Quinn had talked about working undercover. Okay. Bree could do that, too. She would fake her own drowning.

She slowly let herself go limp, knowing she had mere seconds before her lungs would convulse as water filled them and she would die.

Bree acted dead.

Declan released her to float in the water, then he turned her over. She jabbed her thumbs in his eyes. He yelled and released her.

Bree righted herself and rushed the rest of the way to the riverbank—a small sandy shore—but he was on her heels and knocked her to the ground. Turned her over and wrapped his hands around her throat, cutting off the air. She reached for his eyes again, but he kept his face out of reach, his arms much longer than hers.

Darkness edged her vision.

Quinn...

She found a rock, and this time it wasn't stuck in the ground. She threw the rock at his head and it slammed against his temple.

* * *

Quinn yanked Declan's limp but hefty body from Bree. He felt for a pulse. Still alive.

He tugged Bree to her feet and pulled her to him. Hugged her tight. "I was so scared I wouldn't make it to you in time, but even if I hadn't, you got him."

Out of the corner of his eye, Quinn saw Declan pull a gun from his ankle strap and aim it at Bree.

"Watch out!" Quinn shoved her out of the way and to the ground as the gun went off.

He threw sand in Declan's eyes as the other man continued to fire his gun. Quinn tackled him and knocked the weapon away. "You're not getting away with it this time."

Quinn slammed a fist into his face. Man, he'd wanted to do that for a long time. "That should keep you from trying to hurt Bree." At least for the time being.

He helped Bree to her feet again. "I'm sorry about that."

She tried to swipe the wet sand from her face and clothes, but it was no use. "What, saving my life?"

"For shoving you to the ground."

"I'm getting used to it. It's all in a day's work." She smiled as though the weight of the world had been lifted.

But Quinn still carried the burden, the blame, for all that had happened.

Then her smile shifted to a frown. "Quinn, we got him. I heard everything. He confessed to you, and I heard his communications to others. I'm a witness to his crimes. You're going to be exonerated."

"If that's true, then you saved me, Bree. You saved my life."

She peered up at him, and he felt the pull of their

attraction—the deep abiding love they'd always had—and that scared him. He wanted to step back. Step away. Fade away from her life like he'd always done. But he'd taken this risk to end this all for her.

And it sounded like she would be the one to end it for him. It was time to risk love, and he would do it if it meant he could be with Bree. He finally let himself smile, let himself give back to her. He pulled her close to him.

Close enough to kiss. He inched closer, but boats pulled up to the riverbank, sirens screaming, blue lights flashing. The sheriff's marine division.

Sheriff Garrison was among the officers who climbed out of the boat and onto the riverbank.

Quinn released Bree, unsure of what would happen next. He'd done his best. That's all he could do. Quinn's superior, Stan, was with the deputies on the boat. The guy jumped into the river and waded onto the riverbank.

Julia had called him. She'd done everything she had said she would, except protect Bree. "Quinn isn't the man you should arrest," Bree said.

Deputies pulled Declan to his feet and cuffed him even as she said the words.

Stan stepped up to her and shook her hand. "Deputy Carrington, is it?"

"Yes."

"Good work. Julia called me and told me everything to set it up." He then explained that he had been there hiding to watch and listen, unbeknownst to Quinn. He wanted the truth and hadn't announced his presence. Even when Bree had been revealed as a hostage, he'd stayed hidden, not wanting to spook Declan into firing his weapon. When Declan had taken off, Stan had tried to follow, but Quinn had already been in pursuit of Declan. Stan had also called the local marine division deputies for backup along with DEA agents from the local division.

Something wasn't adding up, but Quinn kept it to himself for now. He'd thought Julia had stabbed him in the back, but maybe he'd been wrong about her back there.

"All charges are dropped against you, Quinn," Stan said. "I'll want you back in the New Orleans field office to give me your statement and more details. An informant is passing on the word to Michael Jones that Declan was the one to steal his money, not you, so that should take some of the heat off. And once everything is clear, maybe some counseling is in order before you start your job again."

"I've had a long time to think about that."

Stan's face fell. "You're a good agent, Strand. I wouldn't want to lose you. I'm the one who urged you to lie low for a while, remember? And as the news leaked out that you had stolen money, I didn't want to believe you were guilty, but we put the warrant for your arrest to bring you back so we could protect you as we learned the truth. You didn't have to run."

Quinn glanced down at Bree. He saw what he was thinking reflected in her gaze. Yeah. He did. He was always the runner. But was that really who he wanted to be? Was there another way?

Hours later, Quinn entered the hospital room where Julia was being treated for the gunshot wound. Tears filled her eyes. "Oh, Quinn. I'm so glad to see you. I was so afraid... Declan found us. He shot me and took Bree. I'm so sorry for your loss. I know you loved her."

Bree stepped into the room.

Quinn almost laughed at the smirk on her face, and the shock on Julia's.

"Your negotiation didn't work, Julia. I might not be DEA, but I *am* a deputy, and I know how to protect myself."

Quinn nodded his agreement. "She does, at that. She took down Declan all on her own."

He wouldn't count the gunfire, because well, if he hadn't been holding Bree in his arms, she would have managed without him. He was sure of that.

Stan stepped into Julia's room. "Julia McKesson, you're under arrest."

Quinn pulled Bree out of the room and into the hallway. She turned to him, her face scrunched up. "Somehow, it just seems wrong. She wasn't complicit in most of this. I don't think she had even planned to make any kind of deal with Declan until the end when she was protecting me. She realized this was her chance to get rid of me. Maybe in her line of work, a person could just become calloused. I don't hold it against her. Not too much."

"She gave you up. She gave up both of us."

Bree frowned. "Her negotiation with him meant that Declan would clear your name, and she would convince you that Declan wasn't a dirty agent. I would be dead. Declan would take care of that for her—I would somehow die 'accidentally'—and she would console you. You wouldn't have to hide and could work, and Declan could continue to engage in his double-crossing the DEA and Michael Jones, only he'd use a new strategy. Julia saw it as a win-win. For everyone but me. At least that's how she presented it to Declan. But I don't get the part where Stan was there. She was supposed to call him but didn't because of her negotiation with Declan."

Quinn squeezed the bridge of his nose. "When Declan took you and shot her, Julia decided she would double-cross him in return, and she called Stan to arrange the setup like we had agreed. Turned out that Stan was already on his way to Washington after getting the call from the sheriff about Shepherd taking me and was able to be there in time."

Bree blinked away the unshed tears. "So Declan initially agreed to her plan so she would give our location up, and then when he had his hands on me and shot her, they both betrayed each other."

Julia had taken a huge risk and for what? "She has always been by the book. It's such a shock. Why would she do that? Why would she want you dead?"

"She loves you. Don't you see that?"

No. "I really don't. That doesn't sound like love to me."

"It doesn't to me, either. But she wanted you, Quinn. And maybe that messed up her thinking this through. She said as long as I was alive, you could never be free to love her back." Bree shook her head, obviously struggling to wrap her mind around what happened as well.

Nausea rolled through him. *Why, Julia?*

Stan sidled up next to him. "Are you ready to go?"

He didn't answer right away.

He took in a few breaths to push past the sick feeling. He looked at Bree. She'd grown into the most amazing woman. An outstanding deputy. A wonderful guardian to her nephew, and the best daughter she could be to her father. She was beautiful. Amazing. He'd always loved her but tried to fight it. Even now, he felt his longing for her pull him in her direction. Should he make her promises if he wasn't going to keep them?

"It's okay, Quinn," she said. "I know you have to go. I've always known that."

She planted a quick kiss on his lips, then turned and walked away from him. He almost grinned at that—she would be the one to walk away from him this time.

TWENTY

A month after Quinn left her again, Bree had settled into her life without him like she'd done before. She would be okay. She would survive this.

She made a pitcher of lemonade. The summer had been a hot one, but she looked forward to cooler temperatures soon.

Today they would finally celebrate Stevie's birthday. It seemed kind of strange. Surreal. They were now living in a rental until they were able to buy a new house or rebuild in place of the old home—the place where she'd grown up. Memories rushed at her. Some good and some not so good.

She shoved those bad memories to a grave she'd dug in the back of her mind. It was never good to think about the past or what could have been.

Jayce, Cindy and Taylor were in the backyard with Dad and Stevie.

She set the pitcher on a tray along with glasses filled with ice, and the clinking sound took her mind right back to drinking lemonade with Quinn.

No. She wasn't going to do this today. The counselor the sheriff insisted she see was helping her to let go. She understood Quinn had to go back to Louisiana and assist in cleaning up the big mess Declan had caused. She just wished that Julia hadn't been involved.

Her betrayal had done damage to Bree's ability to trust, though she'd been somewhat wary of Julia to begin with. And Quinn…well, she'd taken the risk to feel for him again.

Risked and lost.

Through the window she watched Jayce and Cindy play with Stevie and baby Taylor.

Her eyes welled with tears. Her heart, too. She could never have that. Stevie would never have that as long as he only had his Aunt Bree.

"Sweetheart, you coming?" Dad asked.

When had he come inside?

He squeezed her shoulder. "I know it's hard, Bree."

She shrugged free and forced him to move when she grabbed the tray.

"Here, let me take that." He took the tray and set it on the counter.

Oh no. Here it comes. A lecture. Just what she needed today.

"I loved your mother dearly. You know that. When she died, I felt so helpless. But I would do it all over again even knowing that she would leave me far too early."

"What? Are you trying to compare what I'm feeling to that? You don't even like Quinn."

"He saved you and Stevie. He brought you back to me. He's not such a bad guy. Look, what I'm saying is that love is worth the risk. Don't be angry at yourself because you love him. It's time you let yourself love, Bree." His grin was mischievous.

"Oh no, Dad. You didn't."

"I did. I invited someone to the party."

"I'm not in the mood for a blind date. Why do you do this to me?"

"I think you're going to like this guy. I have a good feeling about it."

He always had a good feeling about it.

She wished she could like the guys he picked out for her, but it never worked out. She never could feel for anyone else what she felt with Quinn. She grabbed the tray that Dad had set on the counter and rushed out to the backyard, the doorbell ringing behind her.

Must be her blind date.

She groaned inside, but then put on a full smile for her friends and small family. It would have to be enough. Bree poured the lemonade and handed the glasses off to a thirsty crew.

Dad's voice filtered through the house. She cringed as she heard the French doors open. "Just this way. See, we're renting until we can buy another house."

"It looks nice."

She froze. Oh no. Lifted her gaze. Locked with Quinn's. It took her a full thirty seconds to get to her feet. He approached slowly, a tenuous grin on his face and a gift in his hand.

Her father put a hand on Quinn's shoulder. "Bree, I believe you know this young man I invited to the party."

"I hope this is okay," Quinn said, his eyes searching.

Bree must have been giving off a lot of mixed signals because Quinn actually looked uncertain.

"Sure." She cleared her throat. "Of course." Hadn't she been working on letting go? *Dad, what are you doing to me?*

His gaze took in her dress and appreciation reflected in his eyes. She was suddenly aware of how silly she must look in this yellow flowered summer dress.

"You look beautiful." He smiled.

Her heart rate kicked up.

"You look well yourself. Your eyes healed up nicely. No more bruises or scratches."

Stevie ran up to him. "Quinn! Quinn! You came to my party like Grandpa said."

Even Stevie knew about this? Dad must have shown him pictures to remind him that Quinn and his dad used to be good friends, otherwise Stevie was much too young to have remembered Quinn. She glanced behind her at Jayce and Cindy, who had a knowing look on their faces. Apparently, everyone was in on the secret except her.

Quinn handed off the gift.

"Let's open the presents now." Stevie jumped up and down. "Is that okay, Aunt Bree?"

"Okay, sure. We can have cake after the presents."

She was glad for the distraction but felt like everyone watched her and Quinn and not Stevie. At the table, he ripped through the presents, exclaiming joy about each gift, then putting it aside to start all over again.

Quinn's gift came last.

A LEGO *Star Wars* set. Bree widened her eyes. "For a five-year-old?"

Quinn shrugged.

"You'd be surprised what he can put together, Bree," Dad said.

Stevie took his army trucks and played with them on the sidewalk, enamored with his gifts and this special day set aside for him, as every child should be at their birthday celebration. Joy filled Bree at the sight.

Cindy left to change Taylor's diaper. Jayce helped Dad grill forty pounds of burgers.

Quinn just sat there and stared at her. "I didn't mean to make you uncomfortable. Your dad insisted."

"It's okay. It's good to see you. But why are you really here?" She couldn't let him play games with her heart anymore.

"Well, you see, I called up your dad to talk, and then he insisted that I should come."

"I don't understand. You called Dad? That was a huge risk in itself."

"I'll tell you just like I told him. I'm here in Coldwater Bay for good this time. You see, Bree, I was always afraid of being alone. Afraid of losing the one I loved. But that's no way to live."

His hand shook as he drank his water.

What in the world? Quinn nervous? He stuck his hand in his pocket as if reaching for something.

"Here. I brought you a present, too."

He handed over a small wrapped box.

Her heart pounded. She couldn't control the rapid rise and fall of her chest.

"Go ahead and open it."

She wasn't sure she wanted to. "Quinn...without knowing what it is... I... Are you sure? I don't want you to leave again. I don't know if I can go through that one more time."

"I'm staying as long as you want me."

She tore off the deep red metallic paper and with trembling fingers, opened up the black velvet box. "A ring."

"An engagement ring. I called and asked your father for your hand—I figured he was old-fashioned that way, and..."

"You wanted him to like you."

He shrugged and smiled. So cute. So adorable. So...

everything she had ever wanted. He'd made a huge assumption that she would agree to marry him. Showing up here like this, handing off this box. Calling her father. Proposing in front of her friends.

Quinn released a nervous chuckle. Bree wouldn't torture him anymore.

"I can't believe I'm getting married." *I'm going to marry the man I could never forget.*

"Is that a yes?"

She nodded and jumped into his arms.

He laughed and swirled her around. Then when he stopped, he gazed into her eyes. "I won't walk away, Bree. Not again. I can't lose you again. I'm going to protect you and cherish you for the rest of my life."

"I believe you."

Quinn wasn't going anywhere this time. She understood why he was afraid to commit before, but he'd worked through those issues. She trusted that. And like Dad said, Quinn was worth the risk. Now she understood Dad's strange behavior and his little speech in the kitchen.

When Quinn released her, he slid the ring onto her finger. A round of applause from the small group sounded so far away to her ears. She let Quinn kiss her, but not too long in front of the kids or Dad. When he ended the kiss, Bree glanced around. Oh, my...

The crowd had grown to include Quinn's sisters? Their husbands? She looked to Dad, who had a big grin on his face. No wonder he'd insisted on forty pounds of hamburger meat!

The expectation that this would be a celebration put pressure on her. It was a good thing she was nothing but happy with her decision.

"Are you okay?" Quinn asked, holding her hand,

smiling into her face—a man truly in love. She could see that so easily now.

"But…what about your job?" she asked. Life could so easily tear them apart. She knew that from experience.

"I don't have one. I wanted to make sure you wanted me to stay."

Oh. Wow. Okay. He was serious about all of this. "There's an opening in the sheriff's department. They could use a good man like you."

Stevie ran to her and she picked him up. Quinn hugged him, too. Dad smiled, looking on, another part of their little but growing family. She was with all the people she loved now, and Quinn's family had joined them as well. Quinn didn't appear surprised to see them there, which warmed her heart even more.

And she was with the man she had never stopped loving.

* * * * *

If you enjoyed this story, be sure to read the previous books in Elizabeth Goddard's Coldwater Bay Intrigue miniseries:

Thread of Revenge
Stormy Haven
Distress Signal

Dear Reader,

I'm so glad you had the opportunity to read *Running Target*. I hope you enjoyed the story. The characters each had to make some hard choices that I hope you'll be able to relate to, though maybe you haven't been chased by drug runners with machine guns, or maybe you haven't had to choose between your job and keeping someone you love safe. Still, the choices we face every day don't seem all that much easier.

I don't know what I would do if I didn't know how to trust in the Lord. I pray if you don't already trust in Him, that you'll learn to do just that, and soon.

If you'd like to find out more about my books, you can visit my website at www.elizabethgoddard.com.

Many blessings!
Elizabeth Goddard

COMING NEXT MONTH FROM
Love Inspired® Suspense

Available June 4, 2019

BLIND TRUST
True Blue K-9 Unit • by Laura Scott
When guide dog trainer Eva Kendall stumbles on a dognapping, she quickly learns *she's* the ultimate target. But can officer Finn Gallagher and his K-9 partner, Abernathy, help her track down the puppy she's training...and uncover why someone's set their deadly sights on her?

LONE WITNESS
FBI: Special Crimes Unit • by Shirlee McCoy
Rescuing a little girl from a kidnapping thrusts Tessa Carlson from her hideout into the media's spotlight—and a killer's crosshairs. But the child's father, widowed FBI agent Henry Miller, vows he'll protect her from the ruthless criminal who wants her dead.

GUARDING THE AMISH MIDWIFE
Amish Country Justice • by Dana R. Lynn
On the way to deliver her cousin's baby, Amish midwife Lizzy Miller witnesses her driver's murder—and now someone plans to silence her. Lizzy knows better than to trust strangers, but her very survival depends on the help of former Amish man turned police officer Isaac Yoder.

DANGER ON THE RANCH
Roughwater Ranch Cowboys • by Dana Mentink
After her serial killer ex-husband escapes from prison, Jane Reyes has only one person to turn to—his brother who put him in jail. But when she shows up at Mitch Whitehorse's ranch, can he keep Jane and the nephew he never knew about safe?

HIDDEN TWIN
by Jodie Bailey
Amy Brady has been in witness protection for three years when someone threatens her life—and her twin's. Now it's US marshal Samuel Maldonado's duty to get her to safety. But if she ever hopes to be reunited with her sister, Amy must work with Sam to expose a murderer.

PERILOUS PURSUIT
by Kathleen Tailer
Someone will do anything to get Mackenzie Weaver's documentary footage—even kill her. But US deputy marshal Jake Riley won't let anyone harm his late best friend's little sister...especially since he's beginning to wish they could have a future together.

LOOK FOR THESE AND OTHER LOVE INSPIRED BOOKS WHEREVER BOOKS ARE SOLD, INCLUDING MOST BOOKSTORES, SUPERMARKETS, DISCOUNT STORES AND DRUGSTORES.

LISCNM0519

Get 4 FREE REWARDS!

We'll send you 2 FREE Books
plus 2 FREE Mystery Gifts.

Love Inspired® Suspense books feature Christian characters facing challenges to their faith... and lives.

FREE
Value Over
$20

SPECIAL EXCERPT FROM

Love Inspired.
SUSPENSE

*When a guide-dog trainer becomes a target of a
dangerous crime ring, a K-9 cop and his loyal
partner will work together to keep her safe.*

Read on for a sneak preview of
Blind Trust *by Laura Scott,*
the next exciting installment in the
True Blue K-9 Unit miniseries, available
June 2019 from Love Inspired Suspense.

Eva Kendall slowed her pace as she approached the training facility where she worked training guide dogs.

Using her key, she entered the training center, thinking about the male chocolate Lab named Cocoa that she would work with this morning. Cocoa was a ten-week-old puppy born to Stella, a gift from the Czech Republic to the NYC K-9 Command Unit located in Queens. Most of Stella's pups were being trained as police dogs, but not Cocoa. In less than a month after basic puppy training, Cocoa would be able to go home with Eva to be fostered during his initial first-year training to become a full-fledged guide dog. Once that year passed, guide dogs like Cocoa would return to the center to train with their new owners.

A few steps into the building, Eva frowned at the loud thumps interspersed between a cacophony of barking. The raucous noise from the various canines contained a level of panic and fear rather than excitement.

Concerned, she moved quickly through the dimly lit training center to the back hallway, where the kennels were located. Normally she was the first one in every morning, but maybe one of the other trainers had gotten an early start.

Rounding the corner, she paused in the doorway when she saw a tall, heavyset stranger scooping Cocoa out of his kennel. Panic squeezed her chest. "Hey! What are you doing?"

The ferocious barking increased in volume, echoing off the walls and ceiling. The stranger must have heard her. He turned to look at her, then roughly tucked Cocoa under his arm like a football.

"No! Stop!" Panicked, Eva charged toward the man, desperately wishing she had a weapon of some sort.

"Get out of my way," he said in a guttural voice.

"No. Put that puppy down right now!" Eva stopped and stood her ground.

"Last chance," he taunted, coming closer.

Don't miss
Blind Trust *by Laura Scott,*
available June 2019 wherever
Love Inspired® Suspense books and ebooks are sold.

www.LoveInspired.com

Love Inspired®

Inspirational Romance to Warm Your Heart and Soul

Join our social communities to connect with other readers who share your love!

Sign up for the Love Inspired newsletter at **www.LoveInspired.com** to be the first to find out about upcoming titles, special promotions and exclusive content.

CONNECT WITH US AT:

Facebook.com/groups/HarlequinConnection

 Facebook.com/LoveInspiredBooks

 Twitter.com/LoveInspiredBks

LISOCIAL2018